The Miseducation of Riley Pranger

Pepper Pace

The Miseducation Of Riley Pranger

©Pepper Pace Publications
Cover Design: Pepper Pace

ISBN-13: 978-1984010605

Acknowledgements

Special thanks to D. Kavanaugh for fine-tuning my knowledge of Estill County. And as always, tremendous thanks to my Beta Readers.

The Miseducation of Riley Pranger

When all you know is what you were taught by parents and friends that are ignorant to the world, you grow up to be a man like Riley Pranger, a passive racist and chauvinistic. But Riley is going to get a fast re-education when a single black mother rents his home for the summer and he has no choice but to recognize the actions of the people around him.

Stella Burton is a no nonsense, 6-foot tall curvaceous black woman who has no problem with hurting a man's ego. She is opinionated, specifically about a country where she has been single handedly raising her multi-racial son to be a well-rounded black man.

What happens when white privilege is suddenly challenged? When races clash and you mess with the wrong black woman? This novella contains twists and turns and sexiness as well as appearances from Lt. Christopher Jameson, Ashleigh and their children from the novel Beast, Bodie and Shaundea Matthews from A Wrong Turn Towards Love and True from True's love.

Warning: This story includes sexual situations, graphic and strong racist and homophobic language. This story discusses American politics and race relations in a fictional setting.

Author's Note

Before you read this novella, I hope you take a moment to read this note. This story is an IR romance, but unlike any that I have ever written or read. As the writer of the story it has taken me through a roller coaster ride of emotions. There have been days when opening my laptop and continuing the tale has been difficult while other times I cheer out loud, I cover my eyes and cry or I just smile right along with the characters. I have been taken on a journey in writing this story, I kid you not!

If you select this novella, do so with the understanding that it contains a great deal of hate language and the type of hate beliefs that are crippling America. This is a story about what is happening in the United States *right now*. It is a story that drags up emotions that should fuel your outrage about our society. My wish is that this story makes you question and then, to hopefully, seek answers — so that we can all be better people.

I also want you to know that that this is still a Pepper Pace romance and contains my customary HEA, sizzling hot sex, as well as a Pepper Pace twist — its just that along the way you will be shown an America that so many people see and live — and that includes myself. I live in southern Ohio. I work in Northern Kentucky. I have been personally impacted by prejudice. I have been profiled by a white police officer, and more than one white person has called me a nigger.

My readers from other countries may question why I have chosen to write about something so controversial—even people here in this country may ask the same thing. I too get tired of the political back and forth that I see, read and experience in the news and on social media. However, this is *my LIFE*. I cannot be the type of author that writes about interracial issues and *not* write about this. I am a proponent of loving freely, regardless of race or sex. This story promotes that idea.

Still here? Wonderful. Then lets find a solution. Please.

~Pepper Pace~
January 2018

How do we create a resolution? Some people say there can't be a resolution. I'm very optimistic.
                    -Joyner Lucas, Rapper, Activist.

Contents

Author's Note vi
Chapter One..1
Chapter Two 11
Chapter Three..23
Chapter Four..29
Chapter Five...43
Chapter Six 54
Chapter Seven..66
Chapter Eight..76
Chapter Nine..90
Chapter Ten 104
Chapter Eleven 119
Chapter Twelve 130
Chapter Thirteen 145
Chapter Fourteen 155
Chapter Fifteen...167
Chapter Sixteen 175
Chapter Seventeen 184
Chapter Eighteen 195
Chapter Nineteen 207
Chapter Twenty...214
Chapter Twenty-One..225
Chapter Twenty-Two 235
Chapter Twenty-Three...242
Chapter Twenty-Four...252
Chapter Twenty-Five..263
Chapter Twenty-Six 275
Chapter Twenty-Seven...282
Chapter Twenty-Eight..290
Chapter Twenty-Nine...301
Chapter Thirty 314
Epilogue...325
About the Author...338

The Miseducation Of Riley Pranger

Awards 339

The Miseducation Of Riley Pranger

Chapter One

~Summer 2017~

Riley topped the pot roast with the onions, potatoes and carrots being sure not to allow the potatoes to touch the broth. He remembered that his mama had always done it this way so that the vegetables steamed and wouldn't become mushy after hours in the crockpot.

He did this almost every Sunday and it still amazed him that when he returned home later this evening this seared piece of semi-raw meat floating in water would transform into tender roast beef surrounded by thick gray.

He then padded through the neat house until he reached the living room where he sat in the reclining chair to pull on his boots. Riley had two pairs of shoes; the boots that he wore to church and the ones in the entranceway that he wore everywhere else.

He didn't take time to settle into the cushion of the easy chair, which was about as old as he was. Once upon a time he would have never dared to so much as look at it, let alone set his butt on it, although he did recall once taking a

1

dare to do just that once when his parents were out. Afterwards he'd been scared to death that his father would be able to tell. He supposed it's why the chair was still like sitting on a cloud, despite the faded and worn tapestry pattern.

Once he had his boots on he grabbed the keys from the mantle and left the house without bothering to lock up. He didn't recollect the front door ever being locked when he was a kid. If anyone dared break into someone's home the entire mountain would know about it by the end of the day including the identity of the robber. Therefore, it just didn't happen. Everybody knew everybody else up here on Cobb Hill. And everybody knew everybody's business.

He climbed into a dented old Chevy that had basically been pieced together by his own hands, but that purred like a kitten under the hood. He drove in no particular hurry even though the church service started promptly at eleven o'clock, and no one liked being the one to interrupt the service once Pastor Tim started.

Not that the pastor ever worried over it, but it opened you up to the scrutiny of the entire congregation for such things as being late...but not having enough time to iron that dress, or being late...to probably hide that bruise after getting hit upside the head the night before and etc.

The radio was playing a Rascal Flatts tune but Riley didn't pay attention to the music that drifted over the speakers. Much of his life moved in exactly that manner. It was just habit and he walked through it without much conscious thought, like the backdrop of the country music that he didn't particularly have a fondness for, or the smell of pot roast on Sunday, which he enjoyed mostly for the nostalgia.

Once he reached the church he parked his truck and strolled up to the little whitewashed building. He always timed his arrival so that he entered the church just when the doors were closing. And then he slipped quietly into a back pew. This way he missed having to chitchat with anyone including his well-meaning pastor and first lady. It wasn't that he didn't like the people that he went to church with, but he knew that many of them were quick to gossip. Even the most innocent question would lead to rapid speculation about his business.

Riley knew for a fact that there weren't many people in these parts that gave two shakes about him or any other Pranger. Many folks thought that the people living on Cobb Hill were nothing but hillbillies and the Prangers had done a lot to give credence to that belief. But Riley held his head up high just the way his mama had always taught him. And now that his mama was buried out back in the cemetery along with most everyone else in his family all he could do was abide by her teachings even if it meant that he showed up at church alone and barely spoke to anyone.

Pastor Tim began preaching about man's desire to rule over creation. He kept it simple and got a few 'amens' whenever there was a lull in his preaching. One side of Riley's lip tilted upward slightly as he remembered how much granny had disliked Pastor Tim. She'd mutter insults at him *almost* under her breath just because he had replaced old Pastor Mulhaney. The old pastor had been her pastor since she was a girl but he'd gotten so old that he'd forget which sermon he was giving right in the middle of talking.

Riley didn't mind Pastor Tim who talked about books and themes that were broader than what most people on the Hill thought about, although, for the most part he kept it simple.

Riley's eyes settled on a boy in the pew ahead of his that was playing quietly with two Hot Wheels cars and his mind drifted back to a time when he used to do the same, quietly driving the toy cars across his legs and along the back of the pew ahead of him. Sometimes his Mama would give him a warning look and sometimes Granny would confiscate the cars and deposit them into her big black plastic pocketbook. But she'd return them to him a few minutes later and he would smile like it was Christmas. Back then, being able to play with his Hot Wheels while in church was almost as good as Christmas—sometimes better because at times he never got anything at Christmas.

Before Riley knew it the sermon was over and he realized that he had a smile on his face, not because Pastor Tim had timed it to last exactly an hour (verified by most of the men in the church who checked their wrist watches and sighed in relief), but because the little boy had distracted him and for a little while he had remembered a time when coming to church wasn't something that he did alone. He wiped away the smile.

Half an hour later when church was officially over he tried to be the first one out the door but the pastor's wife always seemed to know that was his plan and would make it her duty to 'engage' him. He couldn't just ignore her so he politely waited for her to rush down the aisle toward him.

"Riley. How are you, son?"

"I'm fine." His voice sounded like there was a wet fish shoved down his throat and he cleared it realizing that these were the first words that he had spoken all day.

"That's good," she continued while staring into his eyes the way only well-meaning older women like teachers and pastor wives did. "How's your grandmother?"

As ornery as ever, he wanted to say. "She has some good days…but mostly bad."

The middle-aged woman's slightly pudgy faced took on a look of concern. "When we tried to visit a few weeks back she had no idea who we were…" Riley could tell that it bothered her. He wanted to tell her that it was okay and not to take it personally because sometimes she didn't know who he was and that was one damned shame since he was the only one that mattered anymore.

He didn't say anything and the pastor's wife gave his shoulder a brief pat.

"Well you wish her well for us and take care of yourself, Riley."

"Yes ma'am. I will," he said with a brief nod and then he headed out the door being sure not to make eye contact so that he wouldn't have to speak to anyone else.

A few minutes later Riley parked in the lot of LovingCare Elder Facility located in Irving, a short distance from Cobb Hill. He didn't like that granny lived here instead of on the Hill but she needed constant care and it was something that he could no longer handle alone. His brother and sister were certainly no help. They'd moved out of Estill County their first opportunity. Come to think of it, so had he—only circumstances had forced his return. His mood threatened to darken—not that anyone could tell. His quiet nature had already marked him as moody; a typical Pranger, someone that you crossed the street to avoid.

He went inside and signed in as a visitor, a formality since everyone knew him and knew to expect him each and every Sunday. The woman at the front desk didn't bother to greet him. She had been told long ago that she shouldn't speak to the tall white man with the long beard. He was only in his twenties but he had cold, dead eyes.

Riley went straight to the recreation room where many of the residents spent their days. If the weather was nice they would be out on the front porch in wheelchairs but it was too hot for that even though it was just the beginning of June. He wasn't looking forward to what July would have in store for them, especially working at Bodie's Garage where it was either too cold in the winter or too hot in the summer.

Riley spotted his grandmother's wheelchair in front of the large screen television where some travel show was playing. His heart sank when he saw that she wasn't looking at it but staring at her hands, which were clasped in her lap.

"Granny," he said softly while kneeling beside her. Her head lifted slowly and she looked at him. He offered her a tentative smile. "Hi. How are you today?"

"Who are you?" she asked after a few moments of staring at him.

He swallowed. *I am the grandson that you took to church every Sunday of my life. I am the boy that lived with you along with my mama, daddy, brother and sister in a house built by your husband's very own hands. I am the person that stayed with you when everyone else was gone.*

And I am the person that brought you here when I couldn't take care of you anymore.

"I'm Riley, granny." He stared into her rheumy eyes hoping to see a spark of recognition.

"Riley..." Spoke the little old lady who barely remembered that her name was Jewel. She'd once had sparkling green eyes set in a heart shaped face with skin the color of smooth cream. Her long auburn hair had once been the envy of many women. And she'd been sassy and wild... and

8

now she wasn't. Dementia had turned her into someone unrecognizable both physically and mentally.

Jewel reached out one knobby, wrinkled hand to touch his long beard. He was twenty-seven and having a beard so long that it reached his collar bone was at odds to the young man that he had once been; athletic, ruggedly handsome and outgoing. But that was then and this was now.

Jewel touched his beard tentatively and Riley covered her hand lovingly with his own hand.

"I don't know who I am," she said in a small, lost voice that shook with age.

His eyes stung. "You're Jewel Marlene Pranger. You're my grandmother." *And I love you granny. I love you.*

She didn't seem to understand the words that he spoke.

It didn't do him any good to stay too much longer. She wouldn't remember his visit--but he would. He'd dream about this tonight and maybe over the next few nights. He kissed her on the top of her head when she once again focused on her folded hands.

He saw a nurse watching him sympathetically. The older black woman came to him. He'd seen her before, of course. He knew most of the staff even if he didn't talk to them at length beyond asking after his granny's appetite and health.

"She's having a bad spell today," the nurse spoke.

No shit, he thought. But this wasn't the nurse's fault. "How long has she been like this?" he asked.

"Almost all day."

Riley ran his hand through his short hair. Despite the beard he kept the hair on top of his head short. He was big, taller than a lot of men and still well-muscled even though it had been six years since the last time he'd picked up a football.

"Alright," he said after a time and then he walked away.

When he got home that evening the house was filled with the succulent aroma of pot roast and gravy. The potatoes and carrots were cooked perfectly but he no longer had an appetite. Still, he took himself up a plate of food and then sat down at the dining room table that was more accustomed to being surrounded by a family of eight than just one lone person.

Riley. Where are your vegetables, boy? He could practically hear his grandmother's voice in his ears.

He got up with a sigh and whipped himself up a quick salad before taking his seat and resuming his meal.

Chapter Two

"It's already a done deal, brother. When I get my NTA I'm going to get deported."

Bodie stared at his friend and employee in surprise. "But aren't you one of the DREAMERS? I know the immigration laws are all messed up right now but they aren't deporting DREAMERS yet-"

Pete shook his head slowly. "I told you about how I got busted selling weed back when I was a kid. I don't fall under DACA's rules anymore. It's why I stopped reporting to ICE. I just..." Pete shook his head. "I fucked up my entire life while I was still a kid."

Pete knew that it wasn't just circumstances that had screwed him. He knew that the blame rested squarely on his shoulders. Because of his crime he was no longer under the protection of DACA and had basically gone into hiding.

He took a cigarette from a pack in his front pocket. His fingers were clean, an unusual sight for a mechanic. Bodie's fingers were even now black with grease and engine debris and it was barely eight am.

Pete lit up and inhaled, squinting at his friend through the ribbons of smoke. "I just wanted to let you know what's going down."

"Can't I write a letter or-?" Bodie tried but Pete was already shaking his head slowly.

"The only reason that I'm not in jail right now is because of Theresa and the baby-"

Bodie's heart skipped a beat. "Oh my God, what about Theresa and the baby?"

Pete again was already shaking his head in anticipation of the question. It occurred to Bodie that he had probably already told this story many times before.

"She'll be okay. She'll move in with her parents until we can think of something." He ran a hand through his straight dark hair even though it fell right back into his eyes.

Bodie felt his stomach cave in as it all began to sink in.

Pete was being deported.

Pete was going to leave behind his wife, his baby and his home.

There was nothing that Bodie could do. He felt stupid and useless. His muscles were big enough to fight and defend his friends and family. But how could he save Pete, Theresa and little Jace with only muscles?

He reached for the cigarette from his friend's hand. It had been years since he'd last allowed a cigarette to part his lips but Shaun would understand. Pete handed it over without a word and lit another for himself. Bodie turned to him slowly.

"What if you just take off? I can help you, Pete-"

Pete smiled and it was a true smile where the tension lines that had settled between his brow disappeared for the first time in days.

"Why the fuck do you think I'm on this mountain in the first place? If ICE can find me on Cobb Hill in Estill County Kentucky then they'll find me anywhere." The smile fell from his face. "There is no place to run. I have to go back to Mexico." He leaned against the counter, which was littered with greasy car parts and tools. Grimy work orders were jotted on scraps of paper along with disposable cups partially filled with old coffee. Pete knew that he was going to miss this place. He was going to miss the smell of a gummed up carburetor and the sight of oil that looked as thick as black tar. He was even going to miss towing a wrecked car that had taken a bend too fast and needed to be hauled of the side of a blind cliff—after midnight. And he was going to miss Bodie who had given him a chance without ever asking to see his papers like he was some runaway slave.

"How soon?" Bodie asked while staring out the opened set of garage doors into the rolling hills of the mountain.

"I don't know. I'm out on bail but I'll be getting a Notice to Appear letter to face the immigration judge. I don't expect to go home from there." Pete chuckled to himself and stared out into the beautiful mountain setting. He never thought that he would fall in love with this country-ass place filled with nothing but white faces. But then he'd met Bodie who was part Indian and then Bodie's wife Shaundea who was black and finally his wife Theresa who was as white as Wonder bread, and he stopped thinking about race. He had just settled down and began to live.

His parents had fled to the states from Guatemala along with their three children and despite what most people thought it had never been an easy life. When he was sixteen his mother had passed away from what was surely cancer. She never got it treated due to her fear of deportation. His Dad had died years before in a work accident at a factory where the undocumented were able to work without papers for less pay and in dangerous conditions. His father had been one of the many casualties of an industry that worked every drop of sweat out of you before discarding your used carcass.

His mother and older sister had been domestics and his brother had dropped out of school to work in the same factory that had killed his father. Selling weed had helped to make ends meet and nothing more. Unfortunately, he hadn't been any good at it and had gotten busted before making any real cash. When he hadn't been immediately deported he had vowed never to look at the stuff again. His mother had scraped together all the cash that she could and he had taken off, getting as far out of Texas as he could and had landed in the mountains of Kentucky to a place that he hadn't even known existed.

"How in the hell *did* they find you here?" When the young Hispanic man had approached him for a job, he was barely twenty, broke and hungry. He'd given him a chance, even allowing Pete to sleep in his office for a few weeks until he had enough to get a place of his own. He'd watched him quickly get on his feet. But when he had accepted the Social Security Card that the boy had given him, he'd wondered... Could it have been that? Even after seven years?

"Theresa is convinced that it has to do with the Prangers."

"The Prangers?" Bodie looked surprised.

"Yeah, remember that time Riley and I got into that argument? Theresa said that her uncle was in Stubby's that night and heard him and the rest of the good ol' boys talking shit about me. She said her uncle heard them using the word ICE. The thing is that we don't talk about none of that. And it's not a term that I've ever used in front of her."

Bodie's heart was slamming in his ribcage. *God damned nosey ass, interfering troublemaking Prangers!*

"I don't know shit about Mexico," Pete continued. "I was five years old when my parents brought me and my brother and sister over. My parents are passed on so I don't even really have a contact over there. Plus if my people had money to take care of me then my parents wouldn't have left in the first place." He took another draw from the cigarette. "What the fuck do I know about being Mexican? I grew up thinking that I was just like the rest of you white people," he tried to joke. But Bodie flashed him a quick look.

"I'm a quarter Cherokee and in these parts it means I'm all Cherokee."

Pete briefly squeezed his shoulder and nodded before pushing off the counter. "For a while I forgot that I wasn't actually American."

Pete shook his head and Bodie could see his eyes glisten. "I felt like an American, Bodie."

Bodie had no response to that because these days even he wasn't sure what that was supposed to feel like. "What are you going to do?" Bodie asked quietly. What would he do if someone tried to separate him from all that he knew?

Pete blinked and gave Bodie a half smile. "Learn how to speak Spanish again."

Bodie went back into the office and then gave Pete his final check. It was twice as much as normal. He whispered to his friend that he would send him more once he got into Mexico City. Pete tried to tell him not to do that but Bodie continued as if he hadn't interrupted.

"I want you to find a place to live and to get yourself settled. That check is for Theresa and Jace. I'm going to send you a couple of grand once you get down there. I can't say whether or not any thing of value that you try to take with you won't be confiscated, so better safe than sorry. Contact me as soon as you can. Don't be too prideful, you hear me?"

Pete swallowed and his eyes once again took on a bright and glistening cast. "I hear you Bodie. I didn't come here for that," he continued when Bodie opened his mouth. "But I'll take you up on it."

Pete grabbed the older man into a bear hug. He'd worked for Bodie since he was twenty years old and seven years with a man like Bodie had given him ideas of owning his own shop, of being married and having children and living the American dream. Only thing is that somehow along the way he had forgotten that he wasn't American.

Riley finished up his coffee and then washed the dish and set it in the drain board next to the plate and the skillet that he had used to fry the two over-easy eggs and four strips of bacon that he had each morning for breakfast.

He walked through the quiet house and sat on the worn wooden bench situated by the entrance, to pull on his work boots. They never reached further into the house then this three-foot entranceway unless he wanted to spend the next several hours cleaning grease marks from the wooden floors or the throw rugs.

Since Riley didn't have a wife or a woman or a mother to do his cleaning for him, he had learned long ago that if he didn't want to clean up he needed to make sure that he didn't mess up.

He walked outside thinking that it was going to be a miserable summer if it was already pushing eighty degrees at the ass crack of dawn. He tossed his lunch pale into the driver's side of his truck. In it were roast beef sandwiches left over from yesterday's Sunday dinner.

He turned on the radio and listened to a morning radio show as he drove to Bodie's Garage. He'd done the same thing day in and day out for the last five years. It took no thought to knock the dings out of the body of a wrecked car or dis-assemble and reassemble an engine. Riley hadn't really had to do much thinking since returning to the mountain. And although he hadn't consciously operated in this way, it was the way he preferred it.

He got out of his truck and walked into the quiet garage. He was surprised that the radio wasn't on. Pete usually got in before him and the place would be pumping out some channel from Richmond that played progressive music that made the hair on his skin rise up. Bodie would have the second pot of coffee going since he usually started work even before the sunrise.

Riley plopped his lunch box into the fridge and saw Bodie coming out of his office.

"Hey Bodie," Riley said while reaching for his coveralls which hung on a hook.

"Riley. I need to talk to you."

Riley paused taking the time to look at his boss for the first time. Both men were big but Bodie was built like a professional wrestler. He embraced his Cherokee heritage although he looked like most of the people on Cobb Hill besides his darker coloring. His eyes were grey and his brown hair was filled with red and blond highlights.

Something about the expression on the man's face gave Riley pause.

"What's up?"

"It's about Pete." Bodie said while staring at him.

"What about him?" Riley asked.

"He's getting deported."

Riley didn't say anything as he absorbed the news. Pete didn't like him all that much—a lot of people didn't. They'd gotten into it once before and Riley had called him *Pedro*. Pedro was, in fact, his real name but Riley had spat it out as if it was a curse word and Pete had looked at him differently afterwards, the way some people in town looked at him. It didn't make him no never mind if Pete looked down on him. Riley didn't need to break bread with the man. They just shared a place to work.

"Wow, that's a shame." Riley said slowly. And he meant it. He knew the man had a woman and a little boy. He suddenly thought about all the cars out back that needed working on. Bodie was going to have to hire someone quick and he hoped that he wouldn't think he would take on double shifts. He wouldn't mind doing a little extra but the sign said Bodie's Garage, not Riley's-

"Did you have anything to do with immigration going after him?"

Riley's attention jerked back to Bodie. Wait--? What did Bodie just say? Was he honestly asking him if he'd gotten Pete deported?

Bodie continued, "Because I know your cousin and the people you hang with, Riley-"

"What the fuck, man?" Riley said incredulously.

"You and Pete got into a shoving match-"

"That was nearly a year ago!"

"Look Riley," Bodie growled. "Pete is a good person and he doesn't deserve to be ripped from his home. There's no reason for immigration to be up here sniffing around unless someone said something. Maybe you said something to Sully or one of the others-"

"I don't have to say anything. Everybody knows he's an illegal! He got caught, that's all. Don't make it my fault!"

Bodie looked away. His face had taken on a steely expression. When he met Riley's eyes again they were blank of emotion.

"You're going to have to get up out of here-"

"What?" Riley gave him an incredulous look. "Are you fucking firing me?"

"I don't trust you!" Bodie yelled. "I don't want a sympathizer around me and my family. And after this...I don't trust you." He gave him a final look. "Get your stuff. I'll be fair and give you a week's pay on top of what you earned."

Riley's face turned red in rage. "Fuck you Bodie! Fuck your week's pay! Fuck this job and fuck your family!"

Bodie's expression fluctuated between something that looked like regret and resolution.

Riley stormed back to his truck. When he realized that he was still holding his coveralls he threw them to the graveled ground. He glared at his former boss before climbing into his truck and abruptly starting the engine.

"Sorry son of a whore..." he muttered before ripping out of the parking space with his lunch box still in the refrigerator.

Chapter Three

Riley drove mindlessly until he ended up in front of the little trailer that belonged to his cousin.

Sully came out dressed in just partially zipped jeans and Riley suddenly remembered that it wasn't even nine o'clock in the morning.

"Riley. That you, boy?" Sully called while standing on a rickety porch that held a mix matched set of rusted metal chairs amidst several crushed beer cans.

"Yep." Riley slammed the door of the truck and headed up the porch stairs. Sully stepped aside to let him in. A window air conditioning unit was burring noisily, and along with an oscillating fan situated right next a rickety, second hand armchair the interior was surprisingly cool.

"Ain't you supposed to be at work?" Sully asked curiously. He retrieved two beers from the fridge and thrust one at Riley before opening the other for himself.

Riley felt slightly better with the cold brew and the knowledge that he hadn't gotten his cousin out of bed since the television was turned to ESPN.

"That son of a bitch Bodie Matthews just up and fired me!" Riley exclaimed. He sat down on a couch, which was haphazardly covered with an old blanket. The trailer was filthy, but he was used to it. Unless Sully was hooked up with one of his meth headed girlfriends who might take a notion to pick up a little, the trailer stayed in a perpetual state of disgusting.

Sully stopped in the middle of scratching his scrawny chest.

"Fired? What you do? Look at the ass on his black bitch one time too many?" Sully grinned. He didn't cotton to race mixing but since Bodie wasn't completely white it didn't much matter that he'd taken up with the black girl that he'd knocked up--although it did perplex him as to why he'd up and married her since she was already giving up the goodies.

Riley was scowling. "Get this," and then he recounted the entire story about Pete getting deported and how Bodie had blamed him for it. Sully's expression darkened when his name was brought up.

"That nigger-loving mother fucker brought my name into it?" Sully asked incredulously. Not that he cared whether he was given the credit for having an illegal deported. They could all go back to Mexico for all he cared—illegal or not. But he just didn't like Bodie acting hoity-toity.

Riley swallowed back his beer and felt a little better although he rarely drank except on Saturdays when he met up with his cousin and his cousin's buddies at Stubby's. It too was part of his routine—but only in small amounts. He'd seen how drinking had wrecked the lives of so many people that he knew, including his cousin, which is why he didn't make much time for it.

"He's blaming everybody but the person that should be blamed for getting into this country illegally in the first place," Riley spat bitterly.

Sully went back into the kitchen for another brew. "You can't expect anything different. They stick together--as they should. But that don't mean it's right for him to leave you without a paycheck." Sully returned to the living room and took up his seat in the rickety armchair. "I told you not to trust that asshole Bodie."

Riley hoped that his cousin wouldn't start rehashing his old dislike for Bodie and Shaun. Sully still blamed them for his time in jail for murder. He'd killed Keegan McMichaels in a drug deal gone wrong but hadn't even spent a year at Green River after his appeal went through and he got off claiming self-defense. Keegan did have a violent nature so a long record of violent offenses had contributed to Sully's freedom. Still, he'd taken a good ass whupping from Keegan's older brother Derrick and he'd blamed Bodie for that as well. For protecting Shaundea, who he referred to as 'that black bitch' that he'd unsuccessfully tried to set up to take the fall.

Riley didn't agree with Sully that any of that was Bodie's fault and had told his cousin this time and time again. His cousin should count himself lucky that he'd gotten off with just a few busted ribs, a broken nose and a few lost teeth. But Sully hated Bodie more than he did Derrick who was the one that had beaten his ass.

It didn't make much sense—only it did because Bodie was part Indian and that was enough of a reason for Sully to dislike him. Riley didn't share those thoughts. Bodie had given him a job even after the beef with Sully and he had nothing against Shaun who brought them all cold drinks and lunch whenever she made extra. She'd bring the little girls with her to the garage and Riley thought they were cute the way they grabbed their dad's legs and tried to hug him while he'd raise his dirty hands over his head so that he wouldn't get grease on their pretty pink clothes. His eyes would get big and Riley would hide a grin at the big man's dilemma of wanting to pick up his little girls but afraid of getting them all dirty. Riley would think that if those were his little girls he wouldn't give two shakes about their clothes getting greasy. They'd each get all the hugs and kisses that they wanted.

"Hey, that leaves the spic's girl available," Sully said with a bright expression. "I may pay that bitch a visit," he muttered mostly to himself. "Not that I'd want a girl with a spic baby."

Riley just stared at his cousin in disbelief that he'd think that the pretty, strawberry blonde girl would give him the time of day. Sully still hadn't replaced his missing teeth that had been knocked out by Derrick. And by the smell of him he hadn't bathed in days. His filthy trailer was about all he owned and it was nothing but a haven for empty beer cans and bottles. The ones not empty were filled with black tobacco spit from his chew. Besides that, Sully had never been much to look at and at the age of thirty-six he appeared ten years older than that. And considering that he subsisted on just meager monthly disability and SSI checks he wasn't anyone's good catch.

Riley blew out a long breath. He loved his cousin, would do anything for Sully but he didn't want to hear this shit right now. He stood, leaving his half empty beer on the filthy cocktail table.

"I better get going. I gotta think about my next move."

Sully stood and clapped him on the back. "Alright, cuz. And don't let that prick's action take you down. Bodie Matthews ain't nothing but a piece of cow shit. He got a little bit of something and wants you to beg for his generosity. Well fuck him! Pranger's don't beg. We hold our heads up high! You remember that, Riley. Hold your head up high. That prairie nigger ain't shit!"

Riley stared into his cousin's eyes. His words hadn't made him feel better, only worse. He pulled Sully into a quick hug and then left. The fire went out of him as he walked to his truck, recalling what Bodie had said. He didn't trust him around his family and then Riley had spat out a hateful fuck you and fuck your family…

Chapter Four

Riley parked his truck and sat in his driveway for a few minutes. He lived a lot better than Sully but he also worked hard even though everyone thought that everything he owned had just been handed to him. Sometimes he hated living on Cobb Hill for the way everyone just assumed things about him. If only he could take away all the bullshit and just have the beauty of the land, then everything else would be bearable...

He allowed his head to fall back against the headrest as he made up his mind on how he was going to get the money to hold him over until he could get another job.

Jobs weren't easy to come by on the mountain. You had to go down to Ravenna or Irvine, and still the pickings were small, especially once Kroger had closed. Carhartt was where most families found a way to pay their bills—at least legitimately. But once the weather grew bad, driving up and down the hill each day was no walk in the park. And while there was work on Cobb Hill he needed to bring in more than the pittance that he would earn at the local grocery store.

With a sigh, he thought about the off he'd received for the last two years to rent out the neat little cottage that sat next to the main house. He'd dismissed the offer a year ago when things were going good. He valued his privacy, but beyond that having to rent out part of your home was a reminder of the lean times from back when he was a child and his parents had to do it to make ends meet.

But property taxes were coming due and unless he wanted to sell meth with his cousins he was going to have to do something.

Nobody on Cobb Hill had much money but Riley's family had even less. He had been raised on hand-me-downs from the church's collection box and there had been times when he'd gone to school wearing things that the other kids recognized as being too worn out for even their use.

For generations his kin had been bootleggers and now meth dealers that were too poor and ignorant to do more than try to make themselves feel better at the expense of others.

The Prangers gave a bad reputation to the people on Cobb Hill who were far from rich, but who--for the most part--lived decently and treated people fairly. Riley had always known this about his family, which is why he had never taken to looking down his nose at anybody else. Hell, his family was even too po' dunk to be accepted into the Ku Klux Klan.

He'd turned to football, not thinking that it would be his way out. It had just been a way for him to play with his siblings and cousins — people who couldn't judge him because they were just like him. But then he'd gotten so good that folks wanted him to play high school ball. It was something that he'd excelled at and it made him feel good when he could smash those hoity-toity assholes from Irving and Ravenna that thought they were so much better than him.

He was even more proud when he'd gotten a full ride to Eastern. But he hadn't just relied on the football program. He'd studied so that he could get that college degree that no one in his family had ever attained. College had made a change in Riley Pranger. No one at the university knew what the Pranger name meant and he was judged on his abilities and not on the people that had come before him. The world opened for him and for the first time in his life he realized that he had unlimited possibilities.

A proximal tibia fracture is not words that a twenty-year old man should learn while laid up in a hospital in excruciating pain as a surgeon explains that the bone at the tip of your knee has been broken and that you will never play football again; and not just college or professional ball, but not even for your own pleasure.

Riley had come home knowing that he was here to stay, and all the possibilities that he'd once dreamed of disappeared.

He sat in the truck staring at the big house and the small little house that sat beside it like a fancy, displaced garage. The gingerbread house. Grandpa and daddy had built the little cottage for granny and grandpa right next to the main house so that Daddy could give mama more space without the extended family. Mama hadn't been raised on the Hill but down in Ravenna and wasn't used to living with family all crowded together in one house.

Granny hadn't been too fond of his mother's desire to displace her and grandpa and had complained that she'd raised five kids while living in the house. But she couldn't deny that the cottage was perfect and never complained about it once her and grandpa had moved into it. People always stopped to look at it because grandpa had made it look almost exactly like a gingerbread house just to please granny. People on Cobb Hill took pride in the things they did. His daddy and grandpa had been artisans.

The cottage was what people now called open concept with one bedroom on the main floor and a loft that was often used as a second bedroom. The kitchen was spacious and even had a working 1940s Chambers stove and an actual Frigidaire. The appliances had given him his love of tinkering with old parts just to keep them both in working order.

During lean times mama and daddy had rented out the cottage, forcing Bobby to give up his bedroom and double up with Riley. Granny knew that it was necessary and never complained but he'd once heard her say that it was a damn shame that she couldn't even count on the pillow beneath her head being hers and hers alone. It was the only time that he'd ever heard her show discontent about being poor.

The cottage was mostly rented out to people coming up to Cobb Hill for the holidays. No one liked travelling up and down the mountain during bad weather, especially at night when back then there had been no streetlights. Cobb Hill was notorious for its winding roads and sharp drops.

Life hadn't turned out as planned. His grandparents had never really gotten to enjoy their old age in the cottage. His grandpa had died before that could happen and grandma's dementia had gotten too bad for her to live in the little house alone. Daddy had died and then mama, and a year ago he'd had to place granny in an assisted living facility. Now the property was the responsibility of Riley and at the age of twenty-seven he was still astonished at how fast it had all come to this. He remembered just like it was yesterday their home filled with noise and crowded with people. Now it felt like an abandoned house even though he still lived there.

Bobby and Mae who both had families had scoffed at the idea of moving back on the Hill. And one of the few coherent words that granny had spoken was that she didn't want Sully, Mandy, Angel or any of her many other grand children moving in with their bastard children. That she'd said it right in front of them had resulted in the reason that Riley was basically the only person that visited her in the old folks home.

With another sigh he finally went inside, tossing his keys on the mantle. He suddenly realized that he'd left his lunch pail in Bodie's refrigerator, which only served to irk him once again at being fired over something that had absolutely nothing to do with him. It was like Sully said, the bastard was hot headed and just wanted to punish him because he represented an America that most liberals despised. Would it have made any difference to Bodie to know that he'd voted for Obama? Why should it be anybody's business what his political affiliations were? He kept them to himself. He certainly wasn't going to share them with Sully who thought Obama was a monkey.

The point was that now he was stuck with a hefty debt that had no way of being reduced. The utilities were manageable and there was money in the bank to cover the bi-annual property taxes. But then there was granny's housing cost at the assisted living facility. His brother and sister helped but more and more they found reasons to be late with their share of the payment. Granny had enough grandchildren that it shouldn't be a burden on any one person...but she had alienated most of them when she had referred to them as a bunch of meth heads and their illegitimate children as bastards.

Besides that he had his own medical bills — to the tune of thirty-seven thousand dollars.

He didn't blame the university for not picking up the added costs after his injury. It was him that wouldn't believe the doctors when they told him that he wouldn't be able to play football anymore. He had added on more and more rehab, pushing his body until he'd probably done more harm than good.

He could have defaulted on the bill and none of his people would have thought any less of him. But that was mainly because most of his kin didn't have a pot to piss in. Out of anger or spite or just plain bull-headedness, Riley had made a monthly payment to the hospital without fail.

Reluctantly he searched his desk for the letter that the woman from Cincinnati had sent weeks ago. He'd shoved it there instead of depositing it into the trash like the letter he'd received from her last year.

Her persistence had unsettled him so he had kept it, maybe for evidence. He wasn't sure. He found it squished into the back behind some yellowed receipts that looked like they were ten years old. He removed the letter from the envelope and re-read it.

Dear Mr. Pranger.

I am writing you again in hopes that you will reconsider my offer to spend the summer in your gingerbread cottage. There was an article about it in our local paper and the pictures were amazing. It said that you and your family occasionally rented it out. If you recall, I wrote to you last spring in the hopes that you would allow my son and I to spend part of our summer break there. My understanding is that not only is the cottage a beauty but so is Cobb Hill.

We are, what you might call, city-folk. And as I have no family in the south it is up to me to give my son the experience that so many kids growing up in the urban areas rarely get. Cobb Hill is one of the most beautiful places in Kentucky and it's just a few hours from us.

Of course, we would not inconvenience you in any way. I understand that it has been renovated but still has the same character. We would bring our own supplies, including cleaning and bedding.

School lets out the last week of May and we would like to spend the month of June on Cobb Hill. I'm willing to pay you one thousand dollars for the use of your cottage, if that is acceptable. I look forward to hearing from you.

Sincerely,
Stella Burton

The letter had been written in perfect script and had contained her address, but no phone number. He was a bit uneasy about allowing a single lady and her kid to stay in his cottage.

Besides, Cobb Hill wasn't some campground. There were copperhead snakes everywhere and the Internet was shitty. Everyone had to have a satellite dish in order to watch even regular television.

She sounded like a tree hugger so maybe she would like the rustic life. Well he would make sure that she understood that the deal was non-refundable.

Besides a grand would replenish his savings once he paid the taxes so he shoved the letter into his back pocket and headed out the door to the post office.

Riley got out of his truck, pocketing his keys and walked up the stairs to the post office.

An older black woman was exiting the small building. She used to do the laundry down at the Suds-N-Tan before retiring. His mama had worked there for a while before she got too sick. Riley thought her name was Miss Mabel. He opened the door and she quickly averted her eyes before he could twist his lips to say good morning. His mouth snapped shut and his eyes became hooded as he waited for her to move out of his way so that he could go inside.

Mr. Frank and Mr. Dennis were sitting in wooden chairs chewing the fat with Old man Connors that ran the post office. As far back as he could remember, Riley recalled some old bag of bones sitting in the wooden chairs playing checkers, drinking Coca Cola in the summer and mugs of coffee in the winter. This decade it was Mr. Frank and Mr. Dennis.

They greeted him in surprise.

"Heya Riley," said Old man Connors. "You in here bright and early. Ain't you supposed to be at Bodie's?"

He frowned at the nosey old peckerwood. "I need a stamp." And then he remembered that he hadn't bothered to bring anything to write on or with. His face reddened. "And I need some stationary…and an ink pen."

Old man Connors pushed his spectacles up on his nose and moved from his position where he had been leaning against the counter chit chatting with the two old bag of bones.

"Well do you want a book of stamps or just one?"

"I just need the one," Riley said while slapping a dollar bill on the counter.

"Of course I can sell you an envelope with a stamp already on it and I can give you a sheet of paper but it won't be all flowery like real stationary."

Riley nodded. "I'd appreciate that Mr. Connors."

Mr. Connors passed him the items and then his change. "Only sixty-one cents. The mail don't run for another hour and a half if'n you want to take your time with your letter."

Riley moved across the room to the far counter. "This won't take long." He jotted a quick note to Miss Stella Burton hoping that it wasn't too late. It was already the second of June.

> *Dear Miss Burton,*
>
> *Please accept my apologies for the delay in responding to your two requests to rent my cottage. As long as you understand that the cottage is rustic living with no Internet, Satellite or Cable TV, then it is yours to rent for the dates that you requested. The payment of one thousand dollars is acceptable and is non-refundable. I would require it in full on the day of arrival.*

The cottage is in excellent condition with a recently remodeled bathroom. There is a window air conditioning unit in the living room along with ceiling fans in the loft and bedroom, which keeps the home comfortably cool even during the hottest days of summer.

The kitchen has an old-fashioned stove and refrigerator but no washing machine or dryer. Feel free to use the ones in the main house with no restrictions. If you are agreeable with my terms then I will see you both soon.

Sincerely,
Riley Pranger

Riley dug the envelope from his back pocket and carefully copied down the woman's address. He then handed it over to Mr. Connors who glanced at the name and address before dropping it in a bin to be picked up by the mail truck. Riley wondered if he would reach in the bin and rip open the envelope as soon as he walked out the door.

Well he could snoop as much as he wanted as long as it kept his nose out of his and Bodie's business—not that the news of his firing wasn't probably already making the rounds.

He felt his annoyance begin to once again rise. No. It was more than annoyance. He'd liked Bodie. It hurt that the man would treat him with so little regard--all because of a man that was in the country illegally in the first place.

He left the post office and then because he didn't have anything better to do he decided to go over to Stubby's where he knew the guys would be despite the fact that it was the middle of a workday. But none of them had jobs so that didn't matter.

Chapter Five

Shaun parked next to her husband's truck wondering why there was only his car parked in the lot. She wrangled the girls out of their car seats — it wasn't that easy being that she was eight months pregnant. Nobody had told her to expect that each pregnancy would result in a larger belly than the previous pregnancy. Right now she thought that she looked like a bloated whale. Being a petite 5'5" the added bulk made her feel clumsy but she had to work past that because she had a three and a five-year old to wrangle with. Whoever said that girls were the tamer sex?

"Can daddy go to the park with us?" Myisha, her eldest asked.

"Myisha, you always ask that and I always tell you the same thing; Daddy has to work. Hold your sister's hand."

"Can daddy go to the park with us?" Madison mimicked looking at her mother expectantly with big grey eyes that looked just like Bodie's. Shaun shook her head and hid a sigh.

"No Maddie," Myisha replied in exasperation. "Daddy is too busy."

It broke Shaun's heart to hear her daughter say that—but it was true, which is why she liked bringing the girl's up to the garage to visit with him every so often.

"Go on and find your daddy but don't get in Mr. Pete's or Mr. Riley's way."

"Yes mama!"

"Yes Mama!" And then they ran off hand in hand to the garage. Shaun went to the back of the truck and retrieved the picnic basket filled with food. She'd spent the morning frying fish and making home fries. She'd even made hush puppies because Pete loved them so much. There was also a jug of sweet tea to keep the boys hydrated in this sweltering weather. The garage had central air but that was blown the minute the large doors lifted to allow cars in and out, so mostly it was just relegated to the private office.

Bodie met her at the entrance of the garage with his dirty hands raised over his head as if he was being arrested. A little girl was latched onto each of his legs as he walked using big steps like he was a giant.

Shaun paused wondering how it was possible for her to love him more than she had the moment before. He was everything. Grease

45

streaked one cheek and his forehead and his usually sun-blonde hair was dark with sweat. A beard covered his cheeks which Shaun liked because it made him look like a bear; a toned muscle bound bear.

"Hi babe." He greeted her with a hands-free kiss. "How's my little man doing?" He asked while glancing down at her swollen belly.

"I told you Bodie Matthews that you ain't about to have that son just yet. You better have that little girl's name ready."

He scoffed but didn't particularly mind having little girls that squealed when they saw him and stared at him as if they were looking into the face of God. Being a daddy humbled him. He couldn't love his children more whether they were girls or not.

Shaun had walked into the garage to put down the picnic basket and she looked around curiously.

"Where are the boys?"

Bodie walked to the sink to wash his hands, the girls still clinging to his legs and giggling.

"Yeah," he said. "I was going to tell you about that when I got home tonight."

"Tell me what?" Shaun followed him to the sink when he took too long to continue.

He glanced at her as he scrubbed his hands. "Petes getting deported."

"What!" She exclaimed. "Oh no. Theresa and the baby…"

"I know." He told her what he knew and what he planned to do to help Pete and Theresa.

"Oh this is so terrible." She crossed her arms and rested them on her belly thinking about how alone Theresa must be feeling. She'd pay her visit. Right now she was probably taking every available second to spend with her man.

Bodie finally pulled her into a hug and it felt good having his big body to lean against. He kissed the top of her curly head.

"I know, honey." Pete wasn't just his employee he was family. He rubbed his wife's back until she looked up at him.

"But where's Riley?"

Bodie's lips formed a thin line and then he picked up little Maddie and gave her a bear hug and a big kiss before placing her delicately back to her feet. Then he did the same for Myisha.

"You girls go on to my office. I have a pack of bubble gum in the candy drawer. You can have one each."

Two little voices could be heard squealing in delight as they ran to their daddy's office.

Bodie turned to his wife. "I fired him."

Shaun's eyes widened. "You fired Riley? Bodie, what happened?"

"Nothing happened." Bodie walked to the picnic basket and began digging through it. "I fired him because he's fuc--freaking redneck, wannabe, white supremacist."

Shaun had followed him. "Are you saying that Riley was behind getting Pete deported?"

Bodie had grabbed a paper plate and had a slice of bread on it. He was piling crispy catfish on top of it. "I don't know," he replied. "He said he didn't." He topped his sandwich with another slice of bread and then took a big bite. He told her the story of what Theresa had told Pete.

Shaun was shaking her head in confusion. "I don't understand. You fired him but you're not sure if he had anything to do with what's happening to Pete?"

The girls came running out of the office smelling like cherry bubble gum.

"Daddy can you play with us for a while?" Myisha asked.

He bent down until he was eye level with them both and then he began to tickle them.

"Bodie." Shaun was staring at him with her hands on her hips.

"We're going to have to talk about this when I get home."

She sighed but he was right. There was no talking while the girls were getting their much-needed Daddy attention time. But surely Bodie wouldn't have fired Riley over who he associated with. He was the cousin of one of the most ornery hillbillies on the mountain. But Riley wasn't a hillbilly. She wasn't as close to him as she had been with Pete because Riley rarely let down his shields but Shaun was a good judge of character and she thought that he was good people.

She looked into the picnic basket. "Well I made all this fish-"

"And I'll eat every bite of it," he replied.

"Well...I'm taking the hush puppies home. I can freeze those." Although her plan was to actually cover them with mustard and eat them with a jar of spicy chow chow relish—but Bodie didn't need to know all that. She gave him a meaningful look. "We'll talk when you get home. Come on girls, it's time for us to go so that daddy can eat his lunch while it's still hot."

"Oh man," Myisha whined.

"Oh man," Maddie mimicked.

Bodie gave them a final kiss and tickle. "See you girls at home. I'll tuck you in tonight." He stood and kissed his wife. "We'll talk more later. But I've decided that I don't want people like Riley around me or my family."

"People like Riley?" she asked with a raised brow.

"People who don't take a stand. People who are fine with just allowing injustice."

"You're talking about white privilege?" She asked in sudden understanding. Her brow gathered and she shook her head slightly. "We'll talk about this later." She gestured for her girls. "Come on girls. Time to go. Say bye to Daddy."

Bodie walked them to her car and got them strapped in to their seats, which made Shaun and her baby bump very happy.

"Don't worry," Bodie said while giving her another hug. "It's going to be alright."

How is that possible? Shaun wondered. It wasn't going to be right for Pete and Theresa and Riley was out of a job so it wasn't right for him. And Bodie was now going to be over his ears in work. How was any of this going to be all right?

"I think you should call Riley and give him his job back." Shaun said while standing over Bodie who was kicked back on the couch in just his boxer briefs. He had arrived home just in time to tuck the girls in and he was tired as shit. He had just gotten out of the shower and was not in the mood for this conversation when all he wanted to do was go to bed.

"You're the person that I thought would understand my decision the most." He said.

"Because I'm black?" She smirked. "I live in a southern town in Kentucky. I'm still surprised when I meet white people that aren't out right racist. I've lived my life assuming most white people are at least a smidgen racist." She shrugged. "So I'm not surprised when some white B-list personality is caught using the N-word. Or some redneck city's police chief has a history of arresting more blacks over whites. I am not surprised by this country's level of racism. I'll leave that to the white people who have kept their blinders on for too many years."

"That's what I'm talking about, babe." Bodie said. "I walk into Stubby's and I hear the same rhetoric about Mexicans and the border, about Jews and Middle Easterners. But the difference is that I don't just listen to that shit. I call them on their bullshit. I'm correcting their mistakes when they say something stupid. Fuck, it ain't easy! I'm not a part of 'them' anymore. I'm just Bodie that married the black girl and became a liberal. I am not a liberal. I am as conservative as I've always been but I also can see bullshit and call it bullshit."

Shaun sat down next to her husband and rubbed his tensed shoulders and then she leaned against him and placed her head on his shoulder. His arm folded around her and pulled her in tight while his other hand rubbed her belly.

"I love you so much Shaun. I don't want my children growing up in a world where there is this much hatred."

"Baby, this is the world that we've both grown up in. We have to teach our children what to expect. They have to know that it exists in order for them to be protected against it."

His arms tightened around her as if trying to shield her from the dangers that they were discussing. "I don't want to do that. I don't want them to see this ugliness. They are so innocent and they shouldn't have to know that just down the street someone is going to call them a nigger or an injun or some other stupid word just because of their race."

Shaun sighed. "I had to learn it. You had to learn it. And unfortunately, so will our children."

He didn't say anything for a long time. "Do you see now why I fired Riley?"

She sat up so that she could place her lips on his cheek. "I don't agree with what you did. Riley's always been a hard worker and he's got to take care of his grandmother because none of those other sorry ass Prangers are going to do it."

Bodie frowned. "I could give a shit about Miss Jewel. She's a peckerwood too. She's a white supremacist like the rest of the Prangers-"

"When you hired Riley you told me all about his family history. But you also told me that he wasn't like them. That he didn't use those words and you never saw him join in with his cousins to pick on people. He isn't Sully, Bodie. He's not Sully."

He didn't respond and then he kissed her temple and got up and headed for the stairs to go to bed. Tomorrow was going to be another busy one. He was definitely going to need some help. He had three cars that he was working on simultaneously because the owners expected to drive a twenty-year old car as if it wasn't worth more to just scrap. But that is what he did; he pieced together scraps so that his customers could get as much use out of them as possible.

"Bodie?" Shaun said from her seat on the couch.

"Sorry honey, I need to get some shut-eye."

"What about Riley?"

"Riley can kiss my ass." His frown deepened. "This is a new time in our history. We don't keep doing the same things and treating them like a dark dirty secret because that only perpetuates wrong. The only way to make this world better is for whites like Riley or even me to speak up and take a stand. I told him that I don't trust him and I don't. If he can't take a stand against the wrong he sees in his own friends and family then how can I expect that he won't allow something to happen to you or to my children, that he won't take a stand against that? Fuck him. Sorry for the language but that's how I feel." He went upstairs while Shaun stared until he disappeared.

Yeah, honey. But what if you just pushed him into being just like the rest of them?

Chapter Six

Stella read the letter with a slight smile on her face. It figures that she would hear from Pranger after she had left a deposit on the beach house in South Carolina. It was a nice place, too. Right on the beach with a screened in swimming pool--not that she or her son swam; not in pools or oceans even though the house was just steps away from the sea. There was no amount of water too small or too large that she'd enter that had ever graced another's feet or ass. Swimming was one of many things whose appeal she just didn't understand. To her it was akin to sitting in someone's used bathwater.

She read the letter once again, noting his weak apology and that he hadn't offered to pro-rate the amount or invite her to extend her stay two weeks into July. She sighed. She was just going to have to pay the penalty for breaking her contract at the Outer Banks. Still, she was excited that he'd finally accepted her offer.

Unexpectedly she felt a strange tension in her belly. This was full circle. She had to do this even if she felt like she was about to give a speech in front of a group of strangers.

She pushed the feeling back, silently reminding herself that she was bold and fearless. She scrolled through her smart phone searching for the telephone number to the vacation rental when it began to vibrate in her hand. The name Evan flashed across the screen. She rolled her eyes already knowing why he was blowing up her phone. This was the third call of the day that she hadn't answered and it was barely noon. She had intentionally ignored them because his morning calls were becoming a habit now that it was summer.

He'd understood when she told him not to call in the mornings while school was in session because she was either getting ready for work or already at work. But now that it was summer he was starting a habit that she didn't want. She did not want to talk to Evan every day. He was not her boyfriend. He was not her man.

"Hello," she answered making every attempt not to sound annoyed.

"Hey, beautiful. Everything okay?"

Why did she even answer the phone? That question was enough to push her annoyance level up a few more notches. His real question was, 'Where have you been?' 'Why haven't you answered my calls?' Evan was the type to probe about something or leave open-ended questions waiting for her to fill in the blanks because instead of just being straight-forward he had to try to guilt you into giving him information.

Instead of immediately responding Stella decided to take a few calming breaths. This was exactly the reason that she had always opted to stay single. Small things annoyed the bejesus out of her, specifically things centered around men and relationships. She couldn't handle the little dance that you did with someone new—like the one Evan was doing now. So she tried to politely 'keep it real', even though Evan acted as if they were in a relationship after only a month of dating.

She'd done her part in keeping things casual. Hadn't she kept their sexual excursions limited to his condo so that she could leave immediately afterwards? Didn't she tell him that she didn't want to introduce him to her son? Or maybe he thought that meant for now and not forever...

The thing about Evan is that he was a good catch and deep down she knew it. Her annoyance was just a manifestation of her own lack of interest even though he was everything that the average woman could want. He was beyond good-looking with a deep chocolate complexion, a dark, velvety goatee surrounding amazingly kissable lips. He made good money, had a great job, and lived in a high-priced condo. All of her friends said that he was a good catch so she kept him around, not because she wanted him but because she *should* want him. Only she didn't feel that way about him or any man.

"I'm right in the middle of something. Can I call you back?" she asked, distracted. But she still made sure to keep her voice light and polite as she continued searching for the elusive phone number.

"Well I just wanted to know if you wanted to go out to dinner tonight, you know, before you hit the beach?"

Translation: I wanted to know if I can get some booty before you leave town.

"Sorry. I'm going to be super busy." She placed him on speaker so that she could open an email from the rental.

"Well you have to eat, right?" He continued. Her brow arched.

...with Adam, my son that you've never met...

"Yeah..." She said slowly and distinctly. "But I'll be too busy to go out."

"I could bring you something. I've never met your son."

Stella almost choked. Did this fool just invite himself over to her home-which he'd never set foot in? Did he just suggest meeting he son before she'd ever extended the invitation?

She pulled out the dining room chair and sat down casually and then crossed her legs. She placed the phone on the table. And then she gave her annoyance permission to do whatever it wanted. *Here we go...*

"No Evan. I am busy. I cannot eat with you today, tonight..." *or possibly ever you persistent freak.* "I will call you when things aren't so hectic."

Evan sighed. "Listen Stella. I really like you. I don't feel as if...you realize that. I mean, I'm not trying to toot my own horn, but most women would really appreciate what I'm about."

Now he was calling her unappreciative? This is why she didn't do relationships, she reminded herself as her annoyance changed to real anger.

"I know this is not a good time, but I'd really like to move our relationship to another level." He paused while she seethed silently. Some other woman might feel a special way about his revelation. But she wasn't that woman. She was just preoccupied by the realization that he was still talking after she'd told him *twice* that she was busy.

"Wow…" he finally took the hint when the silence stretched. "I guess you really are busy, or maybe I mistook your interest."

"How is this even a question?" she asked incredulously. "I *told* you that I was busy. And instead of respecting that you just keep…pushing."

Now it was his turn to become silent. When he finally spoke his voice was clipped and angry. "Well, I'm sorry that my phone call was such an inconvenience."

Sarcasm was met with sarcasm when she responded. "Apology accepted. Again, I'll talk to you when I'm not so busy."

"Don't bother," he snapped.

"Okay." *Bye bye now, and good riddance. Have a good life.* She ended the call in relief.

Men described Stella as coldblooded and hard to get next to. She didn't dispute it. She had always known that she wasn't like other people; that she didn't *feel* like other people. She latched onto a few friends and was content with that. Even during college when people went through a sexual awakening she had viewed sex more like something to study and analyze. It was enjoyable, but so was hot chocolate with marshmallows.

Her friends would try to set her up with available men when she just preferred going to the movies or out to eat with a few buddies. But it made sense that she could do that with her own man. So she had gone out on dates but she never felt the way her friends seemed to feel about men. In fact it was kind of annoying the way they always went on and on about their new guy. Men seemed to *change* women. Her friends got stupid and giddy over their men. Or maybe it was the dick that made them giddy. Or maybe she just didn't understand because she didn't particularly care for most men.

Stella wasn't exactly a man-hater. She loved her father, and her son Adam was the most important person in her life. She had wondered if she was a lesbian. She did like her friends much more than she liked the guys she dated, especially when they became pushy or possessive. But Stella realized pretty quickly that she didn't like vagina, so there it was.

She thought that she was maybe a bit asexual. She'd done some research on it and determined that while she enjoyed sex, she wasn't driven by the need for it. After a while, Stella decided that it was because she was just focused. And now that she had a child her interests centered on making their lives the best that she could.

The unfortunate thing is that men liked her. A lot. She was six feet tall—but also thick and curvy. She carried it well...or maybe it was that she didn't lack for confidence, and obviously she didn't desire the approval of the opposite sex. She was comfortable in her own skin. More than one man had likened her to Serena Williams but she looked nothing like her and determined that men just didn't know how to categorize someone like her.

Stella didn't set out to hurt the feelings of these men but they soon learned that she could care less about their good looks, money or the number of notches they had on their belts. After the first disagreement, she would take a physical step back and bid them farewell. And don't play games like try to make her jealous or God-forbid cheat. She just shrugged and went about her business. Stella Burton was tragedy to a man's ego.

Little men were attracted to the idea of being dominated by her, good-looking men liked that she had a blasé attitude about them and they believed that there would come a time when they would control her completely. Fragile men thought to gain strength from her, white men were just a flat no-go and for everyone else she was to be their trophy.

Within an hour she had almost forgotten about Evan all together.

That evening when she picked up her son from day camp she gave him the news.

"Guess what baby. We're going to the mountains after-all."

Adam smiled while pulling his seatbelt across his lap. He was holding onto a drawing, being careful not to wrinkle it. "Are we going to see bears like that time in Gatlinburg?"

"Uh, I hope not." She took the drawing from him and examined it. It was on blue construction paper with pipe cleaners glued to it that looked suspiciously like a boy and his mother. A lopsided yellow sun sat high in the corner and real grass was glued to the ground.

"Is this me?" She asked.

He nodded. "And that one is me."

"I'm very tall," She commented.

"Just like in real-life," he concurred.

"I wish I was this skinny."

He laughed, his crystal grey eyes sparkling in merriment. "Mom, if you were that skinny you wouldn't be able to find any clothes!"

"Well thank you for making me a dress." He had shaped leaves into a fashionable skirt and top.

Adam nodded.

"Are you hungry?" She asked.

"Yeah. We had grilled cheese and tater tots for lunch but I'm still hungry. Can we have chicken curry? They probably won't have good Indian food in the mountains."

"You're probably right," she said as they began driving. She didn't find it strange that her five-year old had a diverse taste in food. From the moment that she'd called him son, Stella knew that she would open the world up for his choosing, and that included exposing him to various tastes and experiences.

He even attended an alternative school that began with toddlers. They were immersed in studies of different cultures, the arts and specifically music. He was no musical virtuoso but he played Twinkle Twinkle Little Star much better than she ever could, and he often dotted his words with Japanese phrases.

She listened intently as he described the day's adventures at day camp while she drove them to their favorite Indian restaurant. Once comfortable in their booth she asked what he wanted to order, as if she didn't already know.

"Chicken curry, spicy three. Aloo-nan and Keema Samosa with extra red chili chutney." She nodded and added Saag Paneer and the two split the meal, finishing it up with no leftovers.

Adam was a robust boy. Some would call him chunky. But he was also tall which meant hat he didn't look like the average five-year old. It was her opinion that his chubby cheeks just added to his cuteness but she knew that one day it might be a problem so she limited his access to sweets and tried to encourage more physical activity. But Adam liked computers and reading and playing video games. There weren't many children his age in their neighborhood and it wasn't as if she could just send him outside to play like in the good old days when she had been a child. Children these days seldom played stickball in the street or hoops against an old building. Or maybe they did, but just not in the suburban neighborhood that she and Adam lived.

It was the prime reason that she wanted to actively do something with him each summer and winter break. Last summer they had gone to Gatlinburg, spending much of it on the Parkway. They usually spent a few days at Christmas with her mom and dad and then off for a week some place warm. They had been to Disney Land, Sea World and even to Washington DC to do a Whitehouse tour.

Some places he might not remember because he was so young, but that didn't matter because she intended to expose and enlighten him to as many experiences that she could.

It went without saying that she loved her son, and he saw not one ounce of the cold disregard that she felt for the adult males of his sex.

"When are we going to the mountains?" Adam asked when they were back in the car.

"You might as well finish out day camp for the week. We'll drive up Saturday morning. She glanced at him, seeing a boy with skin that was nearly as brown as hers but with grey eyes and curly hair that marked him as multi-racial. She was raising a black man, though. Despite those eyes and that hair, America would see a black man. And Stella Burton meant to arm her son with as much knowledge as she could in order for him to navigate this world.

Chapter Seven

Riley heard back from Stella Burton on Friday. He stood by his mailbox and read the short letter, which thanked him and advised that she and her son would arrive Saturday — tomorrow.

Since he wasn't currently employed, he had spent the week making small repairs and getting the place spic and span. He'd been raised by people that didn't scrimp when it came to cleaning. Floors had to be scrubbed, walls wiped down, the stove stripped of every ounce of grease and the tub left gleaming.

He even brought out some of his grandmother's nice dishes from storage and placed a fresh box of baking soda in the fridge.

All he had left to do was turn on the air-conditioner so that the house would be cool by the time they arrived. After that, he hoped they wouldn't be too needy. He had no intentions of babysitting them.

Now more than ever he was a busy man. Job searching hadn't been easy. He'd put in applications and sent off resumes and although he knew that it wouldn't be quick, he had hoped that by now he would have been offered something. He had even sent off a resume for an assistant coach's position at his old high school. And then he was haunted by the memory of how much trouble the Pranger kids had been during High School; getting caught having sex, smoking, selling drugs, etc. Maybe that hadn't been a good move.

He'd heard from Bodie, but only in the form of his final paycheck with a bonus thrown in for good measure. It had only set him off that the bull-headed fool hadn't come down from his stance. Everyone knew about his firing and many of the people on the hill had their thoughts on the matter--and he'd had to hear them as he went searching for a job.

Miss Lemon, who worked at J&B's market, had seen him coming out of the hardware store across the street. The owner hadn't been around but a pimply faced kid had taken the application and placed it behind a counter where it would most likely lay forgotten.

Miss Lemon had left her cash register to tell him that she thought he'd been greatly wronged to be fired all because of that Mexican boy that hadn't even gotten into the country legally.

"Don't get me wrong, I didn't dislike that young man but I knew there was something off about him. I felt it in my bones that he was some type of criminal. I always kept my eye on him whenever he came into the store. But he was very respectful...still, you never know. And now you see what happened." She gave him a knowing nod as if to say that some things were understood and didn't need to be spoken out loud.

"Yes ma'am. Thank you. If you hear about a job opening somewhere would you keep me in mind?"

"They always need a bag boy at the grocery store. I can put a word in for you with Bruce. He's one of the good ones," she whispered covertly.

Riley knew what she meant. Bruce Dunwitty was a kindly African American man that had been managing J&B's Market since he was a kid. But right now with the stigma of Bodie firing him over some unspecified racial activity, he wasn't looking to strike up points with any minority. Especially considering that it was widely known that Sully and some of his friends had repeatedly spray painted the N-word on the front of the store. And not only when they were teens but even after Obama had been elected president— both times.

"Thanks Miss Lemon." He headed back to his truck thinking about his prospects in this economy and specifically in this region. They weren't grand.

With nothing left to do, Riley thought about hanging out with his cousin but it was too hot to sit in the trailer, even with the fan blowing directly on him. And since the only drinking establishment in the entire county were illegal bootleg joints that didn't begin operating until after sundown most of the unemployed watched sports, smoked pot or drank home brew.

He'd always wished for more time to enjoy himself, but even though he was unemployed he was too preoccupied with the manner that he'd gotten that way to find any enjoyment in his new found freedom.

With nothing better to do he went to the library and checked out a James Patterson book that was the start of a series that he had wanted to read. Then he paid a visit to the barbershop. At the most he might be more presentable if he did get an interview and at the very least Miss Stella Burton wouldn't mistake him for one of the Beverly Hillbillies.

He ran his hand through his shaggy hair as Dale; a barber that had cut his grandfather's hair greeted him with his customary 'Ayup.'

Three other men were present but neither appeared to be waiting for a haircut as the second Barber, Bear Musgrove was just sitting in a chair drinking a bottle of Coca Cola.

"You just want a buzz, son?" Dale asked Riley as he draped a crisp white cape over his shoulders, tucking it slowly and securely around his neck.

"Yup." Riley replied. "You can touch up this beard, too," he added.

"Heard you looking for a job." Bear said. He was a burly red head that looked exactly like a bear, only he hadn't gotten the name because of his looks but because his last name was Bayer.

"Looking," Riley said without turning to him. "But not having much luck."

"Hmph," Mr. Epstein said. He was sitting in one of the plastic chairs meant for customers as Dale didn't mind people coming in and shooting the breeze but he only allowed customers — and his other Barbers to occupy the actual 'business' chairs.

Mr. Epstein was old, like most people on Cobb Hill. The young didn't typically stick around, heading for the cities to broaden their prospects. Some, like Bodie, had kin that kept them rooted to the mountain, or there were those that had found comfort and nostalgia in living simply. But mostly people needed to make money to live, so they left.

Riley could see Mr. Epstein giving him the side-eye through the reflection of the large wall mirror.

"Heard the reason that you got fired," he said with contempt.

Riley let a beat drop before responding. "I'm sure there's been plenty of speculation."

"All I can say is that messing with people's lives ain't no joke! You fellas need to mind your business and let others mind theirs! That boy being deported doesn't just mean a loss of a job—it means being separated from his little boy and his girl. I say that's a damned shame!" The old man sputtered out the words, his liver spotted hand was balled into a fist and trembling in contempt.

"Glenn," Dale said flatly, "Riley's here for a haircut, and not here to defend his actions."

Glenn Epstein sputtered. "I don't give a damn! It's a shame, I tell you!

Riley felt his face burn with anger. He knew that a red mask was creeping up from his neck to engulf his face. This was just another indication of what he hated so much about being in a small community. When two of his cousins had gone to Juvenile for busting out car windows down in

Irving, people assumed that he was involved for no other reason than he was the same age and his last name was Pranger.

The same thing happened whenever a Pranger got caught up in something questionable. He wasn't any good because he was one of them Pranger boys that shoot each other, slash tires, and spray painted racial slurs—the sheer definition of poor white trash.

His eyes narrowed as they took in Mr. Epstein through the mirror.

"I don't have any beef with you—yet." Riley said in a voice that was low and menacing. He saw Mr. Epstein's bushy white brows lift. The old man immediately closed his mouth.

Bear cleared his throat. "Well...did anybody watch that tennis match last evening? That Williams gal sure can hit a ball. More athletic than most men I know."

"Sarena?" Dale said while applying the clippers lightly to Riley's head. "I don't think you seen her playing this year. She just had a baby."

"Yeah," Bear said while scratching his perpetual red stubble. "Might have been her sister. But anybody built like that could drop a child and be right back up in Wimbledon."

Riley tuned their forced conversation out as he caught sight of his expression in the mirror. It surprised him enough that it felt like a bucket of water had doused out his flaming anger. He looked like the epitome of what most people thought he was.

He was instantly ashamed of the veiled threat that he'd given to old Mr. Epstein. Why had he done that? Ultimately who cared what the old fart thought? But he didn't have to sound like he might do something to him.

Riley allowed his jaw to unclench and he took a deep breath.

"I didn't have anything to do with Pete being deported. But I got fired all the same." He met Mr. Epstein's eyes. The older man quickly averted them and Riley didn't try again to explain the facts.

"What did you expect from Epstein, that old Jew?" Brady asked while spitting tobacco juice into an empty beer bottle. Sully grunted, they were brothers, Brady older by two years. If Sully was mean then Brady was mean *and* scary. He'd taken over running moonshine for their father who was currently in prison for life after committing crimes that were best not mentioned aloud.

They were cooling their heels at Stubby's along with a few other good ol' boys.

Riley had his elbows propped on the table while he held his bottle of bootleg brew by his fingertips. He took a swig.

"I went in for a haircut. Didn't want any conversation about it."

"Trying to pretty up for that lady that's coming to rent the cottage?" Sully grinned.

Riley grimaced. He didn't want people to start speculating about that on top of everything else. "Nah. I've been sending out resumes." He was hoping for a true to life job interview and not just someone asking him a few random questions about whether or not he'd ever flipped burgers.

Brady interrupted. "Boy, you got that knee injury. That's a perfect opportunity to get SSI disability. You'd have it made in the shade." He finished his brew and then scooted from the table to get another round.

"It ain't much to live off of but there's plenty of ways to supplement your income." Sully said when his brother was gone. "Don't worry cousin. Relax yourself and just take it easy for a while, you know?"

Riley grunted, the beer suddenly feeling like swamp water in his gut. Was this now his life, sitting in a bootleg joint drinking homebrews and listening to Merle Haggard over a jukebox?

When Brady came back he placed a bucket of beer on the table. Frank was the first to grab a fresh bottle. "You peckerwoods are already in for round two." Brady said good-naturedly. "This is the last round so pitch in a few bucks." Typically, each person in the group would buy a round and once that was gone, then the evening of drinking was over. Sometimes when the group was smaller it went into a two rounder, but not when it was after the first of the month, which meant that the government checks were mostly spent.

Brady returned to the previous conversation. "Riley, my boy, the problem with society today is that the bleeding-heart liberals need to make someone pay for the fact that there's a white man in the White House again. You were just a scapegoat. They can't touch President Donald J. Trump so screwing you is the closest thing they got." Riley listened intently. "They want to send a big ol' fuck you to Donald but they can't, so they got you instead."

Riley made a hmphing sound in agreement. On this Brady was most certainly correct.

"Keep America great!" Sully cheered. Everyone clinked beer bottles and cheers of making America great again could be heard throughout the backwoods bar.

Chapter Eight

Riley was in a dead sleep when he heard the crunch of gravel as a car pulled up into the driveway. It wasn't as if he got many guests so the sound was unmistakable.

He jumped up out of bed like a shot out of hell, his eyes settling on the clock on his bedside table, which indicated that it was 8:04 am. *What the hell?* He never slept in like this. Oh right...those homebrews last night.

He hurried to the bedroom window, which overlooked the drive-way where he saw a cream-colored SUV just coming to park.

He cursed and then pulled on jeans over his baggy boxer shorts. He sniffed the armpits of the t-shirt that he'd worn the day before and then tossed it into the laundry basket. Quickly he applied deodorant and pulled on a fresh t-shirt and then pulled on the socks that he'd worn the day before.

He was just heading down the stairs when he heard a tentative knock on the door. He ran his hands through his hair, momentarily surprised that it was mostly gone before remembering his visit to the barbershop. He then stroked his beard reassured that there were no crumbs buried in it. He reached the front door before the second set of knocking began.

He opened it with his mouth poised to greet his new boarder. Instead he stared gaping at a woman that stood nearly eye-to-eye with him, but not just a woman, a young African American woman.

He stuttered in surprise. "Uh...can I help you?"

Stella looked at him steadily before responding. It was obvious why she was here, wasn't it? How many people was he expecting today to rent his cottage? "I'm Stella Burton."

They continued to stare at each other before he remembered his manners. "Oh, right. Sorry..." he gestured over his shoulder. "I just woke up."

"Yes," she said. "I didn't give you a time for our arrival. If you need a few minutes, my son and I can start unpacking the car-"

"I can help you," he said quickly. "I just need to..." he gestured behind him again at the unknown entity that was obviously behind his inability to articulate.

She glanced over his shoulder but didn't see anything. She met his eyes again, trying not to look amused at his total surprise. She'd seen it before, either due to her height her youthfulness or her race. It's funny how white people assumed that she was white just because she knew how to write and speak using proper English.

"I'll get the key and be right out," he said quickly.

"Okay," she turned and heard the door close softly behind her. She had to admit that he wasn't exactly what she had expected, either. She had been surprised by how big and tall he was and although this was Kentucky she still hadn't expected to hear such a thick country accent. He sounded like he'd never been off the side of this mountain. Maybe because he was fresh out of bed but damn, his voice sounded like a cross between a grumble and a soft roar….

After the door was closed Riley stood there a moment blinking. Stella Burton was black.

Riley didn't consider himself racist, that wasn't the issue. But if she understood the situation then she might. He scrubbed his hands across his face and then quickly ran upstairs to brush his teeth and splash his face.

He slipped on his everyday boots and hurried out the front door where the woman and a boy were placing items on the front stoop of the Gingerbread cottage.

The boy, who looked about seven or eight, had been staring at the small house critically. He stopped to watch Riley's approach. He had short cropped-golden brown hair and the most piercing grey eyes that Riley had ever seen on a black person — or in this case a multi-racial person. He wasn't sure just why the fact that Miss (Mrs.?) Stella Burton had a multi-racial child intrigued him.

Riley hurried to help them while discreetly appraising the woman. She was big but in an athletic and toned way. She was dressed casually in jeans, sneakers and a t-shirt that hugged her curvy torso.

Her dark hair was pulled up to the top of her head in a big afro-puff ball that he could barely stop looking at. Also, he couldn't get over her height. It kept his attention riveted in a way that surprised him.

"Keys?" Stella asked as she waited on the stoop with two backpacks thrown over each shoulder. Adam was holding an oversized garbage bag nearly overflowing with towels, pillows and bedding. The man approached carrying the last box from the car propped up on his shoulders...very broad shoulders, Stella noticed.

"It's open, sorry." He should have probably mentioned that the house was unlocked. And how many times had he already told her sorry? He wanted to kick himself — the sight of her just surprised him, is all. He hadn't expected such a young-looking African American mother to rent his cottage. How old was she, twenty-five, twenty-six?

He helped them carry their belongings into the house, flipping on the light to the main room.

Stella's eyes widened in surprise while Adam spun in a slow circle, delight etched across his face. He darted up the stairs to the loft.

"Mom! This is so cool!" he called from the second level.

"Okay…don't lean on that bannister," she said weakly.

Riley smiled to himself. "My Dad and Grandpa made that bannister out of an oak tree. It's as solid as a boulder."

Stella regarded Riley again, still surprised at the countrified hipster with a deep twangy accent. No…he was what hipsters were trying to emulate. He was surprisingly handsome for a man that had a beard that nearly reached his Adam's apple. But it was neat and the moustache curled slightly at the ends so that it looked like he was smiling twice — once with his mouth and the other with his facial hair. He had a buzz cut and she thought he might look better if it was a bit longer, but she had to admit that it all complimented him.

He was tall and big but not like those pro-wrestlers that Adam loved to watch on television. Yet he was still built solid like…well like a mountain man. She turned in order to bring in more of their belongings, or maybe that is what she told herself because she just didn't want to keep looking at him and comparing him to something else.

"Here," he said, moving swiftly in front of her, "Let me get those. You can start unpacking your refrigerator items if you like." She let him lift the heavy crate of food that was sitting on the stoop as if it contained tissue paper. He set it in the kitchen by the sink.

Stella couldn't miss all the homey touches of this cottage. The hardwood floors were old and uneven with cracks and dents but shined like a mirror. The furniture was out dated but nice in a style that might have seemed fancy back in the 50s with a sofa and two over stuffed chairs that had intricately carved legs and beautiful pastel coverings. There was a floor model television that looked like a polished piece of furniture instead of the thin black flat screens of the modern times.

A vase of fake flowers sat on top with...was that a lace doily?

The open concept room was more like a parlor. It led to a kitchen that was so retro that it almost didn't look believable. The sink was a farmhouse style; the web like cracks beneath the old porcelain's patina was a testament to its authenticity. She walked over to the stove and opened the oven.

"It's real." Riley said proudly as if reading her mind. "There's a box of matches on the shelf there. You'll have to use them to start the flame. Other than that it works perfectly."

She moved to the refrigerator and pulled a lever on the door. When it opened it revealed a compartment with a tiny freezer that reminded her of the one that her grandmother had owned. She remembered it having layers of frozen ice that had to be chipped away with an ice pick, or a broken butcher knife.

"These are authentic..." she said in awe.

"Yes ma'am. The appliances are all from either the 50's or 60's."

She looked at him again and this time she smiled. He called her ma'am as if they weren't about the same age. "You can call me Stella."

He nodded. "Alright. And I'm just Riley. And your son?"

"He's Adam."

Adam came into the kitchen. "Mom, the bathtub has feet, like paws!" He looked at Riley, his eyes wide and possibly a little worried. "The outside looks like that house from the book about Hansel and Gretel. An old witch lived in it and tried to murder them."

Riley appraised the boy and decided that he probably wasn't as old as eight; he was just big, big like his mom.

"In the fairy tale the house had candy stuck to the outside. That's how you know this isn't the same kind of house. There are no old witches with magic living here."

"The candy would be melted by now, anyways." Adam said seeming to be relieved.

"I always wondered why that witch would want to eat a couple of kids when she has a house made from all the best candy in the world." Stella said, giving Riley a look of gratitude for easing her son's mind.

"Even witches probably need protein." Adam said with a shrug.

Riley just glanced at Stella. How old was this kid? How old was he when he had stopped believing in fairytales?

"Alright, son. Take your backpack upstairs if you're claiming dibs on that room.

"Okay, Mom." He scooped up his belongings and hurried up the stairs.

When he was out of sight Stella gave Riley a half smile. "He's five and he loves fantasy stories."

"He's big for his age. I was like that too. Going to school being bigger than all the other kids didn't help when you wanted to stay unnoticed."

Stella stared at him as if he was revealing trade secrets. Her expression had gone serious. "You were a loner, Mister—uhm I mean, Riley?"

"Yep." He dug into his pocket and pulled out a large brass colored key with a plastic tag hanging from the end of it. "Here's the key to the house."

"Oh, and I have some money to give you," she said accepting the key. It looked like something you might get if you were renting at the Bates Motel, but she accepted it with a straight face.

He nodded. "I can show you the main house. It's where the washing machine and dryer are located. Then I'll write you out a receipt."

"Adam!" She called. "Come on!"

He darted down the stairs. "This house is so cool, Mom! There is a little teeny door in my room. I knocked, but no one answered."

Riley found himself smiling. He'd done the same thing when he was a kid. His grandpa had pulled their leg and told them it was where the gnomes lived. He'd played many gags on them, even leaving little miniature items around that either he or his brother and sister would discover. Grandpa then made a big production of fussing about the gnomes being messy...that hadn't been a little creepy...He wouldn't trick Adam like that.

"That's a crawlspace," Riley explained. "It's where we keep storage. There's just some old dishes and things in boxes back there." He'd stored some of his grandmother's belongings there as well. He should probably put a padlock on it but the place had stood empty for so long that he hadn't thought about it. Anyway, if the kid wanted to steal a bunch of outdated dresses, shoes and hats then he probably had bigger issues than worrying about gnomes.

As they walked to the main house, Riley pointed out the property line. He explained that Adam shouldn't play by the road as cars took the turns without being able to see. He didn't mention that more than one child had been killed by a person driving blind around the big bend in the roads.

"You can feel free to use the washer and the dryer in the house but the clothes line out back is what most people use, especially with the weather so hot. Your clothes will likely dry in about an hour."

Once inside the main house Stella looked around curiously. It was very neat. She wondered if he was married.

"Do you have any children?" Stella asked.

"No." Riley replied. He looked at Adam. "There are some kids that live on Cobb Hill. The Jameson's don't live too far away and they have a little girl right about your age."

Adam didn't seem impressed. Yeah, he was probably at the age where little girls had cooties.

He led them to the kitchen. "Feel free to use the freezer chest in here. I realize that your fridge is pretty small."

Stella looked around. The house wasn't anything special but she liked it. It was old and worn but very clean. There was a butcher-block table in the middle of the large kitchen with several mix-matched wooden chairs situated around it. It was a table meant for a big family.

For some inexplicable reason she wanted to run her fingers along the worn wood of the table, but stopped herself. She normally preferred modern over traditional when it came to furnishings and designs but the style of both houses was to her liking.

They crossed a faded linoleum floor to a white-washed door. Once opened it revealed a small laundry room. When she saw an old matching gold washing machine and dryer Stella felt as if she was in a 1970s sitcom like The Brady Bunch. A Utility sink was next to it, an old boiler next to that. There was another door that probably contained the furnace. There wasn't a dust ball or cobweb in sight. She couldn't say the same for her laundry room — although hers didn't smell as if it had been recently doused in pine cleaner.

He gave her quick instructions on how to operate both appliances while Adam peered at every single knick-knack in the kitchen — and there sure were a lot of them. She hoped that he wasn't touching anything. Some of the figurines looked old and fragile.

"There's no microwave in the cottage. Feel free to use this one if you like. There are a few pots and pans — mostly cast iron. If you know how to use them they are the best for cooking. I know that when I first started cooking on them I burnt up everything."

Stella smiled enjoying the way he talked and the sound of his country accent. "You do a lot of cooking?"

He nodded. "Not much else to eat around these parts if you don't cook it. There are a few restaurants but they're mostly down the hill. But there is a decent grocery store if you don't need anything fancy."

"You live alone here?" She asked.

"Yep. Since my granny had to be moved to an elder care facility."

"Oh. That's sad."

"Yes," he agreed and then closed the door to the laundry room — and it seemed to that topic.

"I'll get you a receipt for your payment." He led them to the living room where he sat at an old-fashioned secretary. He opened it to reveal a desk area and Adam peered into it intrigued that it had opened like a transformer figurine.

Stella dug into her pocket for the check that she had already made out. He took it, briefly examined it and then retrieved an old receipt book. When he opened it, the pages appeared to have aged but the fact that he had one let her know that renting the cottage was probably something that he did regularly.

"Here you go." He handed her the receipt and closed the secretary. "If you need anything just let me know. The door to the house is left pretty much unlocked. Like I said, feel free to use the kitchen and laundry."

"Oh," Stella said. "What about the Wi-Fi password?"

Riley hadn't thought about sharing his Wi-Fi with renters, but he jotted it down on a sheet from a notepad. Internet wasn't the greatest out here but with his satellite dish he made do. He'd consider whether or not he'd invite them to use the television in the main house. But he didn't really want to walk downstairs and see his boarders chilling in his living room.

After Stella and Adam left the house he stood there for a bit feeling indecisive. Maybe he should suggest some things for them to do...

Naw. He wasn't planning to act as their tour guide.

Chapter Nine

It was Saturday and Riley had a schedule. He generally spent Saturdays catching up on his chores and doing his laundry — only he'd already done all that during the week. Saturday is also when he'd watch some television, catch up on a book or go fishing. Then at lunch he'd head down to Michael's Buffet for the fried chicken, or over to the Whistle Stop and afterwards perhaps get ice cream at the Twin. He'd come home and nap and then head over to Stubby's to hang out with his cousins and their friends.

He decided that since he had a nice fat check, he'd head over to the bank to deposit it before it closed. Riley grabbed his keys and headed for his truck, not worrying about the SUV parked behind it. The driveway wasn't anything but a bunch of gravel and he easily went around.

It was a nice SUV, a late model Lexus. Still, they went for a pretty penny. He wondered what Stella did for a living. Well she probably had some rich ball player in her life, or maybe some high paid corporate type. She seemed the type to date a guy that never got his hands dirty.

He frowned as he thought about his college football dreams. He never allowed his mind to drift to such thoughts. They still hurt. The loss of a dream never completely faded from memory no matter how hard you tried to convince yourself otherwise.

Stella heard Riley drive off while she was exploring the little ginger bread house. Her first impressions of him hadn't been as bad as she had expected. He was polite, even friendly. But he kept his distance and that was something that she completely understood.

She put the food into the Frigidaire and went around admiring all of the nice touches. Adam showed her the little door in the loft and she frowned.

"I don't want you playing in there." The last thing she wanted was for Riley Pranger to get mad because Adam broke something.

Adam just held up his hands innocently. "I am not going into that scary place." He turned his attention to setting up his PlayStation to the miniature television set that she'd allowed him to bring. Luckily so since the television in the living room looked like the last thing that had appeared on its screen was Lawrence Welk or Hee Haw.

I am in the whitest place in America. She glanced at Adam then and felt slightly ashamed. She had learned to temper her strong opinions about whites and America in general. Stella had a few white friends, some of them were even good friends. But whites never really understood what it was to be black.

For the most part, that didn't matter. What did she know about being Asian or Muslim? Nothing. But sometimes the ignorance of white people got in the way. Sometimes she wanted to say, your opinion on something that has never *hurt* you means nothing.

There were times when she almost wrote on her social media accounts 'If you say *all* lives matter one more fucking time, I will delete and block your ignorant ass!'

She didn't allow herself to go there, because she did have a son who was half white. And if she said all that she truly felt in her heart, then she would end up teaching him to dislike that side of himself.

"When we get settled lets go out and explore." She said.

"Okay," he replied, distracted with his gaming system. She knew that he really didn't care about going outside in the heat—not when there were video games and his IPod inside of an air-conditioned gingerbread house.

But she'd done a great deal of research on Estill County, specifically Cobb Hill. And although she was here for more than just a vacation, she still intended to enjoy her summer.

Stella had to practically pull Adam away from his game but once he was outside in the fresh air he looked around curiously.

"I don't see any mountains," he said.

"That's because we are on the highest point of Estill County. Cobb Hill is the mountain."

He gave her a dubious look. "There's no snow."

She placed her hand on his shoulders and smiled. "The word mountain might be a stretch by every day standards. Now let's explore."

"Okay Mom, but there might be bears." Adam said. Although now that he was outdoors he was interested in taking in the sights.

"We'll probably smell a bear before we see it."

Behind the two homes was a cultivated area including an old picnic table, clothes line and barbecue grill made from a rusted barrel. From there they could see a small creek that was narrow enough to leap over...well if you had long legs like Stella and her son. After only getting slightly wet they went on a short hike, being sure to keep the house in their sights.

During her research, Stella had read that these woods led right into West Virginia. She had her cell phone with her but there was no way that she wanted to get lost in them. She warned Adam not to go out alone.

He gave her a look of surprise as if to say that he wouldn't be in them now if it wasn't for her. A squirrel darted up a tree right next to them and Stella ducked as if a bat had tried to land on her head. Adam's eyes brightened in interest.

"That squirrel was so close I could have touched it."

"Well don't. It might bite." She replied.

He continued to stare up at the large tree, craning his neck. "I want to climb that tree. Can I?"

"Okay, go ahead. I'm going to as well." Both discovered that the tree was much too big for them to climb without some type of handholds so they found a smaller tree with branches closer to the ground.

They found themselves perched fifteen feet in the air straddling sturdy branches. Stella couldn't help but think that if they were back at home she wouldn't dare allow her son to do this. But climbing trees in the country was what this vacation was all about.

When they were done with that she climbed down first and then stood cautiously beneath her son as he quickly made his way down, leaping to the ground for the final four feet. He smiled at her proudly.

They explored a while longer, picked flowers, watched birds and rabbits. And once the heat began to cause their clothes to stick to their bodies they made their way back to the house.

"I'm getting hungry." Stella said once they were back at the cottage. "What about you?"

"I'm starving."

"I think we should see if we can find a restaurant close by." She pulled out her smartphone and began a search for nearby restaurants.

"Pizza?" He asked hopefully.

"Yep, that sounds good. Go wash your hands."

A search for a pizza joint was not to be found on Cobb Hill so they drove down to the nearest town. Adam looked around nervously as they made their way down the winding road.

"You just said that you weren't going to drive down this hill again until it was time to leave..."

It was true that the steep hills had made her sweat despite the frosty air conditioning. "If I can navigate through the Smokey's then I can navigate this ginormous hill."

"More people probably drive up to the Smokey's then this road," He said sensibly. She ignored his comment, carefully taking a sharp corner at just ten miles an hour. It was so narrow that she wondered what would happen if another car approached going even a smidgen faster.

She exhaled in relief once they were down the mountain. Even Adam relaxed in his seat. She gave him a wry smile.

"Scary, wasn't it?"

"Nope," he said.

They drove around for a while, not worried about getting lost. The navigation system had gotten them up Cobb Hill the first time with no problems at all and she had no doubt that it would do it again. They past a few pizza joints but after the strenuous drive down the hill they both agreed that a chain pizza joint was not close to a payoff for all the stress that they'd just endured.

They decided on a buffet at a restaurant called Michaels, which had very good reviews on Yelp! It was pretty crowded for just lunch so she knew the food would be good. Once inside she looked around and saw no blacks except ones working in the kitchen. She wondered if all blacks did a similar search when they visited an establishment in an all-white town.

The hostess greeted them and showed them to a booth. She walked with confidence although nearly everyone at some point stared her up and down. She always walked with confidence just for that reason, and also she never wanted her son to see her being anything less.

They checked out the buffet together and Adam gave her a curious look.

"There's no pizza or hamburgers on the buffet. No French fries either."

"That's because this is a country buffet. We eat food like the people in these parts eat." She had no complaints about the selection. There was the standard fried chicken and fried catfish but to Stella's surprise there was also a full Thanksgiving spread including real turkey, fluffy dressing, turkey gravy, and a chunky cranberry sauce. There were also things that she wasn't quite used to such as cabbage and a dish made of green peas floating in an off-white sauce. When she saw others taking up big piles of it onto their plates she dished a bit onto hers but didn't hold out any high expectations.

Even though Adam was disappointed that there was not much of the food that he preferred, it was hard to tell once he began to stuff himself with three fried chicken drumsticks, a pile of mashed potatoes and gravy and a smattering of green beans to appease his mother.

Stella indulged with Thanksgiving in June—and she went back for seconds of the green pea dish.

After their hearty meal, Stella left a big tip—as normal, while the waitress gushed over them and told them to return.

"That chicken was the best! I mean, other than yours…" Adam said.

"Where should we go next?" She asked while looking around.

He paused to squint at her. "Are you scared of driving back up the hill?"

"Nope." She grinned at him. "But maybe we should go to the grocery store again so that we don't have to drive back down here anytime soon."

When Riley returned from town he saw that the Lexus was gone. He was curious about where his boarders had gone off to but then forgot about them as he sank into his reclining chair to watch SportsCenter on ESPN. For the first time since being fired he felt relaxed. A thousand bucks had been deposited into his bank and someone was sure to call him for a job, maybe even as soon as next week.

Even though he had been accused of something that he hadn't done, the people who knew him best didn't care and the ones that judged him wrongly didn't matter. He picked up the Daniel X book and read for a while before dozing off contentedly to the backdrop of a new sportscaster that had been covering high school sports in Texas prior to getting this sweet gig. Maybe life could be so good for him again.

Stella saw that Riley's truck was back in the drive-way when they returned from the grocery store. She and Adam had seen a small market right on Cobb Hill which had lunch meat for sandwiches as well as burgers and hotdogs that she hoped to put on that grill that she'd seen in the back yard. She had even picked up some charcoal briquettes and corn on the cob, which was on sale for a steal.

As usual, she and her son had been met with the expected stares, and although staring was rude, the people were all pleasant. One lady even asked her if she was here to visit Ashleigh and

Christopher — who she assumed was the other black family in the area.

She knew that the teeny refrigerator in the cottage was completely packed with the items that she had brought from home, so she decided to take Riley up on his offer to store some things in the walk-in freezer in the main house.

Carrying paper sacks of groceries, Stella tentatively knocked on the front door before remembering what he had said about the door being unlocked.

She pushed open the door slowly, but Adam barged right in, heading straight for the kitchen with his grocery bag in his arms.

"Hi Mr. Riley," he called casually, walking past the man that had been clearly dozing in an easy chair.

Stella closed the door in chagrin when Riley jolted, a book resting on his chest falling to the floor with a clatter.

"Sorry…you said that it was okay to use the freezer…" Stella said hesitantly.

His look of confusion quickly cleared and he nodded and yawned. "It's fine. I was just relaxing." In truth he had forgotten the offer, but he didn't have a problem with them using the old freezer. There wasn't anything in there anyways except for a few pounds of deer meat.

"I see you found J&B's Market." He said as he spied the brown paper sacks with the familiar logo printed on it. He rubbed his eyes, discreetly checking for bits of grit.

"Yes," she called over her shoulder. "It's a tiny spec but it has everything we're likely to need."

"And Mom won't have to drive down that scary hill." Adam added. Now that he was free of his package he was back in the living room checking out what Riley had been watching on television.

"It wasn't that bad," Stella said as she decided what items she wanted to freeze. Tonight she would grill some burgers and dogs. "Is it okay if we use that old grill out back?" She called.

Riley followed her into the kitchen and was watching as she unloaded her groceries. "Yeah. It's fine."

"We bought our own charcoal and lighter fluid."

His brow lifted. "Lighter fluid?"

"Yeah. You know that stuff to light the briquettes."

"Well, there's some hickory and pecan wood out back. You can feel free to use it. I haven't grilled out in ages so you might as well put it to use. You don't have to use anything to catch it on fire if you use the chimney." Besides why would someone spoil the taste of grilled food with fumes from lighter fluid?

"The what?" She asked in confusion.

"Well it's a," his hands formed a pattern when he found it hard to explain. "If you want I'll just light the fire for you."

She nodded. "Okay. But if you start the fire then you have to join us for dinner."

He shook his head but smiled. "No. But thank you, though. You don't have to do that."

She felt disappointed that he had declined the offer. It would have given her a perfect opportunity to find out more about him. "Are you sure? You could tell us more about Estill County. I did some research and it's very pretty. There's a lot of history here. Plus, we bought a *lot* of dogs and burgers and there was a sale on this corn on the cob."

He took in her hopeful expression and decided that she wasn't just offering out of politeness. "Okay," he conceded. "Thank you." He looked at half a dozen ears of corn still in a paper sack and hid his disapproval. "You don't have to buy any vegetables while you're on the hill. My neighbors give away their corn; they grow so much of it. There are all the tomatoes, beans, potatoes and onions that you can eat. One thing is for sure; a person won't go hungry on Cobb Hill. I tell you what--I'll bring a basket of veggies to add to the meal. Is that okay?"

"Yeah." She nodded in gratitude. Garden fresh vegetables free of charge? What fool would turn that down?

They made plans to meet in the back yard at five thirty to get the grill started. She had to practically drag her son from the television set. He didn't even watch sports but he was standing in front of it just because there wasn't a flat screen television in the cottage.

"Come on Adam. Let's go." She said while waiting at the front door for him to follow.

Riley followed them to the door. "See you at five thirty," he called in his lazy country drawl.

Stella looked behind her and grinned and then she stopped. Why was she grinning like a fool?

"See ya," she called.

Chapter Ten

For the first time in a long while, Riley didn't make plans to spend Saturday evening at Stubby's drinking with his cousin. He got showered and then took a few moments to appraise his newly trimmed beard in the mirror, happy that he'd gotten rid of all the shag.

He went over to Mrs. Carson's place. She had been friends with his mom and was his closest neighbor. She gave him tomatoes, zucchini and squash. He saw that she had a tree with some loose branches or what they called 'widow makers' so he whipped out the chainsaw and took care of that for her.

Riley had plenty of lettuce at the house but he thought some cucumbers would make for a nice salad so he headed over to Mr. Pike's farm and came away with that as well as some big roasting potatoes and a crate of apples. In return he promised to come out and look at his tractor, which kept shooting out black smoke.

As he prepared the salad and sliced the zucchini and squash he found himself smiling and looking forward to getting that old grill going. He remembered being a kid and his dad tending to the grill after getting scraps of a freshly slaughtered pig from a neighbor. Grandma would then take the head and boil it with spices and make souse or take the feet and pickle them. The chitterlings would be boiled and then fried in bacon fat. To others, these things--as well as the pig ears and tongue--were scraps but to them it was a special treat.

He heard Stella and Adam in the back yard. He checked out the window and saw that she was carrying a platter filled with meat while Adam was carrying a box loaded with buns and probably condiments.

He hurried outside to help them, moving the old picnic table beneath one of the large trees. A caterpillar might drop down from a branch but it would shield them from the still hot sun.

"I think we got enough meat here." She said while placing the tray on the table.

"I think so," he agreed in amusement. There were half a dozen over-sized hamburger patties, a dozen hot dogs and a large rope of Kielbasa sausage.

Stella watched as he loaded the bottom of the barrel grill with pieces of wood from a neat pile beneath a tarp situated under the porch.

"Each type of wood adds a different flavor. Hickory can be kind of strong. I like the pecan best," he explained.

"Really?" Stella said in surprise. She never considered that different wood would add different flavor. Adam took over adding the wood and then helped Riley find kindling to add to a chimney fire starter.

"You just gotta find some dry twigs and leaves to add to the bottom and then we'll put some briquettes on top. We'll light the bottom and once the briquettes turn white hot on the edges we'll add them to the grill." Riley explained to Adam.

The little boy was interested at the prospect of helping to burn something and was happy that Riley let him catch the kindling on fire. Adam looked over at his mother who was staring at him in warning that he better not get too comfortable with it.

They followed Riley into the house while the fire got going and he showed them the vegetables that he'd gotten.

"Oh wow. Let me give you some money-" Stella began.

"No. I got all this for free. That's how we do on the mountain. When there's extra we share." He handed Adam a medium sized green apple.

"These are real good. But check for worms," he said just as Adam was taking a bite. Adam froze in mid bite and frowned. He placed the apple on the counter.

Riley chuckled. "I checked for wormholes but sometimes you miss them at the stem. It won't hurt you," he joked. "It's just a little added protein."

Adam's face showed his disgust at that statement and Stella couldn't help but to laugh as well.

"You ever had grilled corn on the cob?" Riley asked them.

"I heard about it, but never tried it." Stella said. Riley noted that she was now dressed in a pretty sundress that flowed around her legs just above her knees. She also wore sandals and had toe nails painted with pink polish. He wondered if she was aware of the snakes in these parts. Most women didn't wear sandals and he told himself that was the reason that he was so interested in the sight of her nail polished toes.

Stella watched as Riley placed several ears of the corn that she had purchased on the grates at one end of the large grill.

"You aren't going to take those green leaves off?" Adam asked referring to the husks.

"Nope. It's insulation. Also it's going to allow the corn juices to steam inside."

He got a wire grill cleaner and now that the grates where hot he used it to quickly clean them. Next to the corn he placed potatoes. Stella placed the meat down while on the 'vegetable side' of the grill Riley added the sliced zucchini and squash.

"You can grill those?" Adam asked curiously as he watched with interest.

"You can grill basically anything." Riley replied. He enjoyed Adam's interest. It had been a long time since someone had been in the house and for the first time in a long while it felt like the home he remembered from his childhood. It took people to make a house a home.

Stella had to admit that the smell of the food being cooked by the pecan wood was amazing, much better than the aroma of lighter fluid soaked charcoal. Riley took over the grilling when the flames threatened to engulf their food. He expertly flipped and moved the meat from one part of the grill to another while casually tending to the vegetables and holding a conversation with them.

"Have you always lived here on Cobb Hill?" she asked.

"Yep. I was born right here in this house. My granny delivered me in the master bedroom. She did the same for my brother and sister, too." He didn't mention that when grandpa died he had been laid out right in the middle of the living room in his casket. By the time that his parents had passed away they had done things at a funeral home and granny had fussed about it until she was allowed to tend to the bodies.

The food didn't take much time to cook and when it was done they ate at the picnic table.

They talked but not as much about Estill County as they talked about themselves. Riley learned that Stella was a teacher at Adam's school where Adam was being taught how to speak Japanese. They, in turn, learned that Riley had gone to Eastern State University to play college football but had left after a knee injury.

Stella had noticed that he walked favoring one side and while she had already known that Riley Pranger had gone to Eastern and had left abruptly she didn't know that it was because of an injury. She knew a little about him, but she wanted to know more and she had no intentions of moving forward until she did.

Riley was getting ready to suggest lighting the torches since it was now dusk, when the back door of his house opened and a man came strolling out. Stella saw that Riley looked more than a little stunned but then he quickly recovered as he hurried over to greet the man with a hand slap and a side hug.

"Hey cuz," Riley said with a smile and yet his expression was still perplexed. "What are you doing here?"

Sully and his kin rarely paid visits to Riley's house, mostly out of a tradition of being unwelcomed by granny. Even though granny had been off the property for over a year the habit stuck. Plus, Riley kept to his routines, which didn't include an appreciation for unannounced visitors.

Sully peered out into the yard. It was growing dark, yet it was still light enough to see that his cousin had been sitting at the picnic table chewing the fat with a black woman and a tubby black boy.

"Who's that?" Sully asked.

Riley gestured uneasily to Stella and her son. "This is uh...Stella Burton and her son Adam. They're renting the cottage for the summer." Stella was peering at them curiously while Adam was deciding whether or not he wanted to take a chance on one of the apples sitting in the basket on the table.

"Well I'm here because you weren't at Stubby's and you didn't answer your phone," Sully said in a loud voice, which meant that he was more than a little wasted. "I came up to check on you. You always show up at Stubby's on Saturday."

Riley patted his pocket, realizing that his phone was sitting on the kitchen counter. He needed to get Sully out of here. Regardless of Stella and Adam's race, Sully never needed to be in polite company. Besides, Riley could smell the home brew on his cousin's breath. And although he wasn't quite weaving on his feet he was obviously inebriated. If he didn't get his cousin back down the hill before nightfall it wouldn't be safe for him to drive in his condition.

"Look," Riley said in a low voice. "I'm helping my boarders." He tried to lead his cousin back into the house. "I'll get with you tomorrow sometime-"

Sully moved past him. "You got all that food over there and I ain't ate dinner." He moved to the picnic table ignoring Stella and her son while grabbing a plate.

Stella's brow gathered. The scrawny man was drunk as hell, but more importantly he was being rude by not even acknowledging her or her son.

Stella noticed Riley sigh, his face becoming stony as he followed the man back to the table.

"Stella, Adam, this is my cousin Sully." Sully barely glanced at them. He began to load his plate with food. Riley hovered next to him as if waiting for him to finish up and leave.

"Riley," Adam said. "You ever grill an apple?" The young boy was examining the apple in his hand for wormholes.

"You don't grill 'em." Sully was the one to reply. "You put 'em in the ash. Bury them and put hot coals over 'em. They taste like warm applesauce. It's a poor man's apple pie, right Riley?" Sully laughed.

"Yeah." Riley said simply. It was obvious to Stella that Riley didn't want the man there and it made her a bit leery.

She stood. "Well it's getting late. It's about time for us to head on out."

Riley said nothing and she found that she was a little disappointed that he didn't object. The conversation had been nice and she was learning a lot. Not to mention the fact that his voice was soothing and made everything feel chill and relaxed. He could probably read the phone box and she'd listen intently.

"Mom. I want to put an apple in the coals." Adam complained.

"We'll do it next time." Stella began gathering the paper plates and plastic cutlery and Riley was quick to help her.

"Yeah, next time, buddy," he said.

Sully stopped in the middle of adding ketchup to his burger. He looked at Riley and then at Adam.

"Go on. Let the boy put an apple in the ash. It don't take that long." He put down his plate and picked up an apple, then he went to the grill and using a stick he lifted one of the grates. "Right there."

Adam followed and placed his apple carefully on top. Sully handed him the stick. "Now bury it. Yep. Just like that. Get it all covered. Careful now. Don't let those red fairies sting you."

"Red fairies?" Adam asked looking up at him curiously.

"Those are the embers. They bite mighty hard." Sully buried the second apple next to Adam's not being nearly as careful and getting bit by several red fairies although he didn't as much as make a yelp. He returned to the picnic table where Stella and Riley were standing awkwardly. "Go on back to the house and get a set of those tongs so we can pluck them apples out of the coals." Sully instructed his cousin.

Riley didn't move. He just stared at his cousin as if he didn't understand. Stella looked from one to the other uneasily.

"Hurry up Riley before the apples burn!" The older man said with a frown. It seemed to snap Riley out of whatever reverie he was in. He turned and jogged the short distance to the house, favoring his bad leg. The fact that the act of jogging was obviously painful to him supported a suspicion that he didn't want to leave the man out there with them.

Sully took a seat at the picnic table and peered up at Stella. "How you like the house?"

She nodded politely while crossing her arms in an unconscious protective manner. "It's a very nice house."

Sully grinned. Stella saw that there were several empty places where teeth once had been. There was somewhat of a family resemblance between the cousins although Sully was a head shorter, making him even shorter than her. His thin, wiry muscles did little to cause him to appear anything but scrawny. He did, however, have the same grey eyes as Riley and his hair was long enough to touch his shoulders. It was a shade of blonde making her wonder if Riley grew out his hair would it be the same color.

"Riley tell you that our grandfather and his daddy built that little house?"

"Yeah, he just told us the story a few minutes ago." It had been built for his grandparents; unfortunately, they hadn't had much time to enjoy it. She relaxed a little although she didn't feel particularly comfortable around the man. But it wasn't like she could leave since they were all being held hostage by the apples roasting in the ash.

Adam, who was oblivious to the conversation, was using the stick to poke at the coals. Even though he knew that he probably shouldn't be anywhere near the hot grill he was going to take full advantage of his mother's preoccupation.

"Our grand pappy and Riley's daddy built that son of a bitch completely by hand." Sully continued. Stella stiffened slightly. "Y'all probably the first blacks to ever set foot in that house. I know that old bitch granny sure didn't take to you Negroes and neither did our grandpa. Riley's daddy weren't too fond of none of you, either, although granny thought Riley's mama was a bleeding heart. That's because she didn't mind working right next to you people. 'Course some folks can't tell the difference between right," he glanced at Adam, "and wrong."

There was a prolonged silence as Sully took another bite of his burger, a satisfied smile on his face.

Adam was now watching with wide eyes, shocked by the bad language the man had just used. He had called his own grandma the 'B' word and that was really bad.

Stella's heart was pounding in her chest but she didn't allow her eyes to move away from him for even one second. *Let's do this...*she thought as her hands formed tight fists.

"Adam," she said casually. "Start carrying the food over to the house." She glanced at the long stick, the hot grill grates, even the apples as possible weapons...

Adam made no protest as he picked up the tray of meat. Sully quickly grabbed another burger and a dog with his bare hands and that's when Riley returned, holding the tongs and looking out of breath as if he'd had to hunt for them — or as if he'd sprinted in order to prevent his ornery cousin from doing something rude.

The very moment that Adam was out of ear shot Stella placed one hand on her hip and spoke in a calm — almost casual voice.

"First, you uneducated redneck, there is not one thing *wrong* with my son. Two,"

She barely got that word out before Riley turned to his cousin. "Sully what did you do?"

Stella continued, this time rolling her head on her neck. "What you need to know about those so-called *Negroes* that the people in your family don't like," her eyes flitted to Riley whose own eyes were as large as saucers, "Is that being liked by poor white trash was probably not nearly as important to them as you white people seem to think." She smirked. "In fact, here's a little secret. Nobody cares what trash thinks."

Sully took another bite of his burger, not appearing in the least phased by Stella's remarks.

"Now this gal, I like." He grinned at his cousin.

"Sully!" That one word carried rage that Riley seldom allowed himself to generate against his own kin. He grabbed his cousin by his upper arm and jerked him to his feet, surprising the drunken man that his younger cousin had set hands on him.

"What the hell are you doing?!" Sully shouted.

"You need to get out of here. Now!" Riley roared. Sully struggled against the bigger, stronger man but he was no match for the painful grip that Riley had on his arm.

"What?" He cried as he was practically dragged to the back door. "Over some niggers? You gonna do me like this?"

"Shut your mouth!" Riley growled while yanking him up the porch stairs. He had forgotten the pain in his knee in his anger. "You don't talk like that in front of my guests! In *my* house!"

"Your guests?!" Sully yelled back, struggling to get out of the bigger man's grip. "You forget who you are, boy?! You a Pranger. I seen you from the kitchen cozying up to those niggers!"

When he'd driven up in his old pick-up he'd seen the Lexus SUV parked in the driveway. The first thought that he had is that some classy hoity-toity bitch from the city was here spending up her alimony money on vacations in the woods. She'd obviously gotten the Lexus in a divorce decree or perhaps she was some rich guy's kept woman. Because to someone like Sully a woman couldn't possibly have worked hard and gotten a nice car on her on. His only hope is that Riley would get some classier pussy than what most Prangers ended up with.

But then he'd seen who the owner of the Lexus was. And his disgust had nothing to do with how Riley was acting for he didn't see him doing anything more than eating and talking. But it was the sheer fact that a nigger had a Lexus. A nigger was driving a better-looking car than he would ever drive. And worse then even that, is that he had been tricked into thinking that she was classier than the women that he associated with. It was this that had angered Sully Pranger.

Chapter Eleven

The two men crashed through the back door. If it had been built by men lesser skilled than their grandpa then it would have come right off its hinges. Riley slammed the door behind him but not before he saw Stella storming off towards the cottage. Shit.

Sully tried to swing on him, but he was slow and drunk. Riley pushed him away in disgust.

"Why in the hell would you do something like that?!" He asked in pure confusion.

Sully had landed on his narrow backside onto the floor. He jumped up prepared to fight the bigger man, because in his eyes Riley would always be that little kid that had tagged around him since he was only knee high. In his drunken state he truly thought that he could take the younger man and teach him a lesson or two. But he cared about the kid and wanted to understand why he was being attacked for basically no good reason.

"Why are you siding with them niggers against me?" he asked in earnest.

Riley closed his eyes briefly. "Don't say that word again." He looked at Sully. "Those are my boarders. You just..." Riley shook his head while staring at Sully in disbelief. "Do you have a thousand bucks to give me now because you've chased that lady away? You got even half of that to put on the property tax? What the *fuck* is wrong with you?!"

Sully quieted and then dug his hands into his pocket. Riley's words were sobering. He'd just fucked with his cousin's money and that was the greatest sin that one man could commit against another. You could fuck his wife, run over his dog or even take the last bottle of beer from the fridge. But one man never fucked with another man's money. Ever.

"Damn. Riley..." Sully ran his hands through his hair. "I'm sorry, man. I was fucked up. I wasn't thinking. I'm sorry, man, really."

Riley's nostrils flared as he breathed but he didn't speak.

"You didn't do anything wrong, Riley. I was wrong." Sully suddenly looked sober as he stared at the wall to one side of his cousin. "My...my own grandmother didn't think I was good enough to set foot in the gingerbread house." He gestured weakly in the direction of the cottage. "Them two boarders of yours can rent the place but I was never even allowed to set foot in it when I was a kid. I guess that always made me want it more. I always thought that I'd grow up and granny would figure out that she actually gave a shit about me after all." He looked at Riley. "But we both know that ain't never happened."

Riley looked down at the aged linoleum floor and felt the guilt that he'd lived with for so many years flare back to life. He knew why Sully ended up the way he had. If things had been just a little different then he could have ended up just like him.

He looked at Sully and saw the blossoming of bruises forming on his arm where he'd grabbed him and the sight was like a blow to the pit of Riley's stomach. No. He was not the type of man that would do something like that to Sully. He would never be that kind of man. He refused to be that type of man.

For a flash he was seven years old and he saw Sully standing here in this very kitchen as a sixteen year-old boy and his Uncle Lloyd was in a boxer's stance slamming his fists repeatedly into the skinny boy's face. Sully's eyes were swollen closed and blood was streaming from his mouth and broken nose. He was barely conscious but the blows came so swiftly that they practically prevented him from hitting the ground.

Not any kid of mine, you little faggot…

Everyone had stood and watched—including the adults, and not one person had put a stop to it. Afterwards granny had been the one to clean up the blood including two teeth, which she had dropped into the trash bin without a word.

No kid of mine…

At six years old, Riley had vowed that he would never be like the other Prangers and he would never do anything to cause his cousin to ever be hurt again.

Riley sighed and reached out carefully towards Sully. The idea of the man shrinking from him would kill him, but Sully was still contemplating his own past memories.

"Come on, cuz." He placed his arm around Sully's shoulders. "Let's get you to bed. You can sleep it off in the spare room."

"I'm sober, Riley." Sully said, but allowed himself to be led to the stairs and to the spare bedroom. "Besides. I ain't staying no place that I ain't welcomed."

"Yeah, well it's too dark to be taking Cobhill Rd this time of night. You'll go down tomorrow." They were silent for a few more moments. And then Sully turned to peer at the younger cousin that had been more like a little brother to him.

"Hey, you still pissed at me?"

"Nah," Riley said. "You're my blood. I can't stay mad at blood."

"That's right. Blood is thicker than water. It ain't tighter than money, though." Sully chuckled and Riley fixed his lips to form a smile. "Sorry for messing with your money. I guess I wasn't thinking. You go on and make that money, black, white, red or yellow; the most important color is green."

"Don't worry about it. I'll take care of that."

"I'll apologize if you need me to-"

"Uh, no."

Once they were in the neat bedroom that had once belonged to Riley, Sully kicked off his boots, stumbling in the process. Riley reached to right him but Sully just fell onto the bed with his pants still on.

"Go ahead and get comfortable. There's beer in the fridge." Riley said while turning to leave. But no sooner were those words out of his mouth than Sully jumped to his feet.

"Well whyn't you say that while we were in the kitchen?"

Stella was still pacing when Adam came downstairs, a full half an hour after returning to the cottage.

"Mom. Do you think those apples are ready yet?"

"What?" She asked giving her son an incredulous look.

"I want my roasted apple," he replied. "That man that called his grandma that bad word said that it's like apple pie."

She stopped pacing and knelt down on the floor on one knee in order to look him in the eyes.

"Adam. Do you understand how rude that man was?"

Adam hesitated before nodding, and then he shrugged and finally he shook his head admitting that he had no idea. All he knew is that his mother was suddenly mad but it wasn't at him, so while her anger was bad, that part was good.

Stella studied him silently, considering what she would do next. There would be many teachable moments in her son's life. But was this one of them? He was just four months from being six years old and he didn't understand what had just happened. Maybe that was a good thing.

What finally made up her mind was her reaction to the situation. She'd allowed that man to get the upper hand. She'd allowed him to do to her what she had vowed that she'd never allow a white person to do, and that was to get a rise out of her.

She sighed. "That man was so rude to come barging in to our picnic and eating our food without first asking. There were just enough burgers and dogs left for you, me and Mr. Riley to have leftovers, but then that man took a hot dog *and* a burger!"

"And then he took two more! Yeah. He didn't ask first. And did you notice that he smelled like he spilled wine all over himself. I bet he was drunk."

Stella stood and placed her hands back on her hips. "And what do you know about that, little man? When have you ever seen a drunk person?"

"I see drunk people all the time on television."

She went into the kitchen and dug up a small saucepot. "You are going back to watching Sesame Street," she muttered under her breath. She then headed for the door. "Wait here. I'm going to go get those apples…"*which is proof positive that I'm not intimidated by a bunch of hillbillies.* She backtracked hillbill(y). She still wasn't sure about Riley. He had been pretty pissed. And when the N-word was used he looked like he was going to beat the hell out of his cousin. Still, Stella was convinced that all white people were racist in secret. And in private places where no one could hear they all used those kinds of words. These thoughts were almost unconscious to her because these were the thoughts that were always a backdrop of her mind whenever she was around friendly, laughing white people--that today they were buddying up with her but yesterday they were probably calling her a nigger behind her back.

Stella once again silently reminded herself that she could never really trust a white person, which is why she had never desired to date a white man. She was convinced that in the back of a white man's mind was a history of bigotry and no matter how apologetic they *sounded*, they had to feel that there was a sense of *right* that they were on top of the food chain—without once taking responsibility for the fact that they had lied, raped, stolen and tortured in order to get there.

While Stella Burton didn't hate white people, she certainly didn't trust them.

The backyard was dark when she returned. The only light was coming from the windows of the main house. It was ridiculously dark in the country where there were no streetlights and even the moon and stars didn't provide enough illumination to allow her to see. She blinked, trying to get her night vision adjusted and thought about running right smack into a bear. To hell with that hillbilly, she wasn't scared of him, but she sure didn't want to run into a bear.

She stumbled over a thick patch of wild dandelion and cursed under her breath. Now that she was out here she realized that this was stupid. Those apples were probably nothing more than mush by now. But it was the principal of the thing. She had to do this.

"Stella?"

She bit back a surprised yelp and then she made out the figure of someone by the picnic table. She blinked a few more times and saw that Riley was holding a garbage bag and cleaning up.

"I just came for those apples. My son wants them," she said flatly.

"Sure. I'm very sorry for my cousin's behavior. Sully doesn't represent the people on Cobb Hill, or me, for that matter."

Now that she was at the grill she could see him clearly. She located the stick that had been used to lift the grate from the grill.

"You don't have to apologize for another man." She said in a clipped manner. She used the stick to carefully roll the roasted apples into the pot.

"Well I do. When you're on my property you're protected by me and my rules."

She looked at him...*protected by him and by his rules*... He said it like that was supposed to mean something to her. Did that mean that it was okay to be a racist as long as you didn't act like one on his property? How in the hell was that supposed to mean anything to her?

"I just want you to know that I'm sorry that you had to face something like that while you were here and I hope that it won't cause you to want to leave. You're welcome here." He meant every word. It wasn't about the money. He liked that someone was in the house next door. He even liked Stella and Adam. It had been so long since someone had been around and he found that after getting to know them over the last few hours that he liked them.

"I'm not planning on leaving." She said defiantly.

"Okay, good." He added quickly, "There're plenty of vegetables left if you want to take them-"

"No thank you," she said simply. "Goodnight."

He watched her walk away.

It was clear that she was pissed, but Riley could see that it was more than that. She was also hurt. He didn't know what Sully had said before he'd gotten to the back yard, but it involved her son and while witnessing good people being hurt was something that he didn't want to be a part of, what bothered him most was that Stella seemed to almost expect it. She wasn't surprised that this had happened. She knew it would.

"God damn you, Sully." He muttered as he tossed the leftovers into the trash.

Chapter Twelve

Riley was just putting the finishing touches on the pot roast when Sully came into the kitchen carrying his boots in one hand.

"What are you doing?" He asked as he sat down in one of the wooden chairs, an unlit cigarette hanging from his lips.

"Finishing up this pot roast for after church," Riley replied.

Sully leaned back in his chair as if the act of coming down the stairs had been tantamount to a days work.

"Is there anymore of that coffee I smell?"

"Yep." Riley gestured to the coffee pot. "Help yourself. I'm leaving in about half an hour if you want to eat. There's some bacon and fried eggs on the stove."

"Mmm!" Sully said happily.

He took the plate minus a greasy paper towel back to the table along with a mug of black coffee. He looked around as he scooped his breakfast into his mouth.

"You living pretty good out here."

"I make do." Riley poured himself a second cup of coffee and returned to the table where he had sugar and a container of powdered non-dairy creamer. He added a liberal amount of both causing Sully to grimace.

"Easy, cousin. Do you even taste the coffee?"

Riley shook his head. "Nope. I'm not much of a fan of the stuff." But he had brewed a pot with the thought that Sully could use it in order to get moving. He had no intentions of leaving the man up at the house while he was away. Not with Stella and Adam nearby—and even if they weren't.

Sully had never asked to move into the cottage. But one day he would and that might be the day that their friendship ended. Because Riley had no intentions of going against his granny's wishes to never let any of them live on the property. It wasn't a respect thing, although he loved his granny. But he'd seen what Sully's family did to property.

Riley took a long drink of coffee and then placed the mug into the sink. "Hurry up and eat. We're leaving shortly."

Sully grunted and Riley went up stairs to finish getting ready. A few minutes later when the men stepped out of the house they both looked over at the cottage.

Sully ran his hands through his greasy hair and stared at the beautiful little cottage.

"I sure made a mess of things for you." He said softly.

Riley climbed into his truck. "Don't worry about it. It's taken care of. I spoke to her last night."

"Did you tell her that I'm sorry?" Sully asked while peering in at Riley through the window.

I don't need a man to apologize for another man... "No. But I told her that I was."

Sully nodded and then looked once again at the cottage. He got into his truck with its fading Confederate flag emblem covering the back window. It started with a loud rattle and a shot of black smoke and then he was speeding down the hill.

Riley sat in his running truck, fiddling with the radio until the clock indicated that church was due to start in less than fifteen minutes. He rolled off, checking the rearview mirror where the gingerbread house was in plain view. He watched its reflection grow smaller as he drove.

Stella looked out the window once she heard Riley and his cousin's cars drive off.

Asshole.

Riley had let that man stay in his house all night. What had happened to protecting them when they were on his property? She tried to dismiss them both. She wanted to forget about the events of last night. She decided that she would make pancakes and bacon for breakfast. Her surroundings even inspired her to make it from scratch although she generally used a box of Bisquick when at home. Why not? You could make just about anything pastry related using Bisquick.

The night before, they had eaten the apples with a scoop of vanilla ice cream. She had to admit that it was surprisingly good and had not gotten as mushy as she had expected. She had even sprinkled a bit of cinnamon and brown sugar on them and it really was like apple pie.

Afterwards Adam had tried turning on the television set in the living room but all of the channels that came in clear were off line for the evening. So they had turned in early with Stella promising that they would explore the mountain the next day.

It was late in the day when they finally left the house. Adam tried bringing his Gameboy along but Stella nixed it.

"Nope. Leave it here. We're going out to enjoy nature."

"So you're not going to check your Facebook?" he asked.

"Don't be smart."

"You want me to be smart." He said while flashing her a dimpled grin.

"Yes, but not a smart aleck." She lightly pinched his cheeks. He was just too cute.

The scenery was beautiful, the trees were in full bloom and if it weren't for the fact that it was blazing hot out she would have suggested that they go on another hike. Instead they saw a creek and she found a safe place to pull off to the side of the road.

They walked down the slight incline and came to a small lake.

"Ooo! Mom, there're fish! Can we go fishing?"

She was happy that he'd found something to interest him. "We sure can. I think that hardware store across the street from the market might sell some fishing poles." Not that she knew the first thing about fishing. Well she knew you had to have a hook, those round floating balls and some bait. Yeah, that would be a good past time. In the mean time they skipped rocks, or rather they threw them causing big 'plops' and splashes.

They located another tree to climb and discussed how cool it would be to have a swing that swung right over the lake. And then there were all the 'what if' questions; what if the rope broke? What if you broke your leg and no one was around? What if you drowned?

"What if nothing happened except you had the best time in the world swinging over the lake?" Stella finally said. "Let's head out. I'm getting hot."

Adam had collected a pocketful of rocks that he liked and an old piece of tree branch that he swore was a witch's petrified finger.

"Then why do you want to keep it?" She asked as they headed back to the car.

"Because it's going to be my charm to ward against evil."

"Evil? You've been playing too many fantasy video games."

"I'm going to tie a piece of rope around it and wear it like a necklace." He announced while holding it carefully.

"Yeah and it's dirty."

He wiped it gently. "No. It's clean. Can I keep it?"

She shrugged. "Yes. You may keep the petrified witch's finger."

He made a few gestures in the air with it and then pointed the 'finger' at her.

"What are you doing?"

"I'm including you in my protection spell."

She smiled and chuckled. "You have such an imagination."

As they drove they came across a small church sitting on a hill. Several cars were parked in front and the doors were thrown wide open allowing them to hear the sound of yells and shouts even from the street.

They were louder than the Baptists, she thought.

"Why are those people screaming?" Adam asked while peering out the window as they drove past.

"I think they are just shouting out their prayers."

She saw him point the witch's finger at the church. *Jeez, I'm going to hide that thing.*

They continued to drive and Adam turned up the Bruno Mars tune playing on the Satellite radio. They were singing along loudly when she thought she saw something that interested her.

"Is that...?" She abruptly pulled the car over and parked. She dug into the backseat for her water bottle.

"What?" Adam asked.

Stella got out of the car. "Come on. Follow me." Adam followed his mother as she walked back along the side of the road. It was one of the few places that actually had a spacious area off the side of the road to park the SUV.

"Where are we going?" Adam asked. There was nothing to see but the side of a huge hill, which looked as if the road had been cut out of a mountainside. The ground was dirt and pebbles along with a few flat rocks that appeared to have fallen down from the side of the hill.

Stella pointed to a spot on the side of the wall of rocks. Adam squinted until he saw that the ground was dark and wet here. And then he saw that a trickle of water was flowing from a spot in the mountainside.

"I think it's a natural spring." She said.

Once they reached it they saw that there was a pipe jutting from the side of the mountain.

"Where's it coming from?" Adam asked. "It didn't rain yesterday."

Stella pointed up. "From there. It's the top of the mountain."

Adam stuck a finger beneath the stream. His eyes widened in surprise. "It's cold. How did it get so cold when it's so hot outside?"

"The mountain top is cold. Should we drink it?"

Adam was unsure but tempted. "Is it clean?"

"Yes. It's naturally filtered. They put this pipe here for people to access it. Or at least that's what I read. Let's try it."

"Okay." He held out his hands to catch the water but Stella stopped him. "The water is cleaner than your hands. Drink it like a water fountain."

"So I have to be the taste tester?" He asked.

"Yes. You first. Someone has to drive you to the hospital if it's poisoned," she joked. He waved his witch's finger at it. "Now it's safe." Then he drank. He didn't stop for a long time. When he did he sighed and smacked his lips. "Good," he said shortly before going in for round two.

"Okay stop hogging it up. My turn." Stella said. Adam stepped back and Stella bent and drank. The cold water hit her lips and she opened her mouth allowing a flood of icy water to fill her mouth. It was so good that she wanted to call it sweet. She dumped the water from her water bottle and began filling it with the frigid spring water.

"I'm going to get my water bottle!" Adam sprinted back to the car as a dark SUV pulled up behind her. She straightened and shielded her eyes but all she could see were tinted windows. The window facing her on the passenger side began to glide down and she saw the face of a light skinned African American woman peering back at her.

"Are you okay?" the lady asked in concern.

"Oh. Yes, we're fine. We saw this spring and thought we'd stop for some water."

Both doors opened and the woman stepped out. From the driver's side a huge white man stepped out as well. He dwarfed the woman especially when he walked around the car to stand next to her.

They made an odd couple, but Stella had no doubt that they were a couple. His hand went around her shoulder as he smiled in greeting. The woman had light skin and short hair pulled back into a ponytail, which sprung out in soft curls around the scrunchy. They were both attractive but the man looked like he could have modeled for…well for anything. He was probably the whitest man that she'd every seen with pale freckled skin and short, curly auburn hair along with a few days growth of a moustache and beard. His eyes were also very light so that you couldn't help but to look into them. It should not have all gone together so perfectly and yet it did. He was gorgeous. But so was she.

"Daddy, can we get out of the car?" A little voice called from inside.

The man's eyes scanned the area, locking onto her car and then to Adam as he jogged back to her.

"Yeah, baby," he said, his smile returning. The back door opened and a little girl stepped out. She looked to be about six or seven. A moment later a little boy followed.

The woman walked toward her with her hand held out.

"I saw you pulled over at the side of the road and wondered if you were having car problems. Cars always stop running on this hill," she chuckled. Stella shook her hand. "Oh, I'm Ashleigh and this is my husband-"

"Christopher!" Stella quickly filled in.

Ashleigh's head tilted. "Do we know you?"

"No," Stella chuckled. "I'm sorry. We were at the market yesterday and the lady working there asked if we were here to visit Ashleigh and Christopher."

Ashleigh laughed. "Right. Because all black people know each other."

Chris moved to lift the little boy up into his arms. He looked to be about two years old. The little girl was light in coloring like her dad and had the same light eyes and long auburn hair. But the boy was brown, even darker than his mom with brown curls and hazel brown eyes—but he looked just like his dad. Stella understood why people stared at her and Adam because she couldn't stop staring at the little family.

"This is Chris Jr.," the man said with an accent that sounded exactly like Riley's. "And this is our daughter Brianna." Stella shook the man's hand. Even though she was pretty tall, her hand felt like it was enclosed by a baseball mitt.

"I'm Stella Burton and this is my son Adam. We're here vacationing for the summer."

"Oh nice!" Ashleigh said excitedly. "We do the same thing. We stay with Chris's mom for a few weeks each summer. Our place is right up the road off Patsy. It's the big A-frame. Where are you and Adam staying?"

"We're staying in the little gingerbread house on the Pranger's place." Stella replied.

The smile fell from Chris's lips. "The Pranger's house?"

"Yes. Well, the cottage."

Ashleigh clasped Chris's hand. "Riley's a good guy."

"Hmph." Chris said shortly.

"What?" Stella asked while looking from one to the other.

Ashleigh smiled. "My husband doesn't get along with a few of the Prangers."

Stella's lip twisted mirthlessly. "Yeah. Can imagine." She looked at Adam. "Go ahead and fill your water bottle, sweetheart." Brianna followed him. Once he was at the water pipe Stella turned her attention back to Christopher and Ashleigh. "I met his cousin, Sully last night."

Ashleigh and Chris exchanged concerned looks.

"Do I need to go and whup his ass?" He growled. Ashleigh placed a placating hand on his forearm. Stella smiled in appreciation at the offer.

"No. I handled it." She frowned to herself. "Besides, I think Riley might have done it already."

"Riley isn't like the rest of them." Ashleigh said. She looked up at her husband. "Right Christopher?"

He grunted. "He alright. For a Pranger."

As the grownups chatted Adam appraised the girl. He'd seen other multi-racial children at his school. Sometimes they passed each other in the halls and even though they had never met it was like they knew each other. It was like that with this little girl. He knew her because they were both in an exclusive club of being black and white but being truly neither. It wasn't something that other black people understood. Even his mother who was the smartest person in the world didn't really know. She said that he was black but sometimes the black kids called him whitey and the white kids asked what he was. If he said black they said that he wasn't. If he said that he was both sometimes they said that he couldn't be white if he was black because white had no colors mixed in...

He filled up his water bottle as the girl watched and then he drank a long swig.

"You want some?" He offered the bottle to her.

"Yeah," she nodded. "We're almost home but my daddy saw your car and thought you got a flat tire or something."

She accepted the bottle and drank. "It's good," she gasped when water dribbled down her chin. "Cold." She handed the bottle back to him.

"My mother says its because it's water from the mountain."

Brianna nodded. "This is one of the places where the spring comes out. We come here with jugs. My grandma sometimes make ice tea just by sitting it on the back porch with tea bags inside."

"You don't need hot water to make it?"

"It gets hot. Then grandma puts sugar water in it and pours it over ice. It's good."

"We had some roasted apples last night. It tasted like apple pie. We put it over ice cream."

"You ever had home made ice cream?" Brianna asked.

"No."

"We make it and put berries and fruit inside. It taste better than store bought."

"Do you live here?" Adam asked.

"No. We just come out and visit my grandma. And we visit my grandpa and uncle Walt and uncle Ray and a whole bunch other people that I never met."

Adam frowned. "How do you visit people that you've never met?"

Brianna smiled. "We visit them in the cemetery. Each grave is like their own little house. I knock on their gravestone and say, 'Hello grandpa. How are you today? It's me Brianna and we're visiting grandma.' Then I tell grandpa all the people that I visited."

Adam dug into his pocket for his witch's finger and showed it to her. "You should get yourself something like this. It will protect you from the evil spirits."

Brianna poked at it. "That's cool looking. But my daddy protects me from the evil spirits, me and my mommy and brother and all the people in our family. He's a Marine."

Adam looked at the huge man. "He looks like a wrestler on television."

Brianna nodded. "He can fight better than anybody on television."

"Adam," Stella called. "Would you like to visit with the Jamesons? They invited us to their house for lunch."

Adam nodded enthusiastically while Brianna clapped her hands in excitement at the prospect of making a new friend.

Chapter Thirteen

Riley strolled into the church and sat down in an empty pew in one of the back rows. As Pastor Tim preached Riley's mind wandered. It bothered him that Sully had said those things to Stella. It bothered him that Stella had been angry at him even though he'd been nothing but nice to her. Although he understood that she needed someone to focus her anger at, it didn't seem right that it should be at him when he had been the one to apologize. Plus he hadn't been the one to use the N-word. He despised that stupid word whether it came from a white or a black person. The last time he'd used it was in college and the circumstances were special. He hadn't ever thought to use it again.

Pastor Tim's words began to infiltrate his thoughts and he stopped thinking for a moment and began to listen.

"Listen to the Wisdom of Solomon: 'For the waywardness of the naïve shall kill them, and the complacency of fools shall destroy them.' Proverbs 1:32. Let me give you two symptoms of complacency: 1. Satisfaction with the way things are. 2. Rejection of things as they might be."

Riley frowned to himself and silently repeated those words. *Satisfaction with the way things are. Rejection of the things as they might be...*

Pastor Tim continued and Riley listened.

"Look at Revelation 3:14-16. 'And to the angel of the church in Laodicea write: The Amen, the faithful and true witness, the Beginning of the creation of God, says this: I know your deeds, that you are neither cold nor hot. So because you are lukewarm and neither hot nor cold, I will spit you out of my mouth.'

"The middle ground is actually the lowest ground. Do you see that?" Pastor Tim exclaimed among a chorus of 'Amens'. "Jesus says I would rather have you hot or cold but I can't stand lukewarm. I would rather have you love or hate but I can't stand indifference. Jesus hates the middle ground. Look at what the verse says. He is saying I would rather have you too – hot or cold – I hate lukewarm. I would rather have you love or hate – I despise indifference. The middle ground is the lowest ground, brothers and sisters."

Riley's attention was fine tuned throughout the rest of the service. Even when the chorus sang and the testimonies began, Riley watched and listened intently. For the first time in a long while he felt as if he'd gotten something from being at church.

After the service he went up to Pastor Tim and shook his hand. "Good service, pastor."

"Why thank you, Riley." He slapped him lightly on the back. "You staying for the church picnic?"

"No sir. I'm going to visit my granny."

"Why don't you take her a slice of pie, and one for yourself? She liked Birdie's lemon pie."

Miss Birdie did make the best lemon pie in all Estill County. And granny had tried getting the recipe but Miss Birdie never revealed it. She wouldn't even purchase the ingredients on Cobb Hill out of fear that someone would reveal the ingredients.

"I'll do that. Thanks Pastor." Riley ended up chatting with a few people as he got two huge slices of pie boxed up.

Mr. Dukes placed an arm around his shoulder as he grinned. "How ya doin' Riley?"

"Doing fine Mr. Dukes. And yourself?"

"Good as gold. Hear you looking for a job."

"Yep. Know about any prospects?"

Mr. Dukes leaned in and whispered. "Well we need someone to run some moonshine from over in Alumbaugh. You can make yourself a pretty penny and help us out."

Riley looked at him in surprise and then abruptly shrugged Mr. Dukes arm from his shoulder. He walked away. He had a lot of God damn nerves asking him to run his moonshine! Would he have said that to one of them Ravenna boys? No, he wouldn't have. He headed for his truck with his head down, effectively avoiding any more conversation.

When he got to LovingCare he saw his grandmother sitting out on the covered porch along with a few other residents. When she saw him approach her face lit up into a broad smile.

"Riley! This is my grandson," she announced. "Isn't he handsome? He was a professional football player before he got hurt. It was a dirty tackle. They were out to get him."

Riley grinned, ignoring the others who were watching him in interest. Seeing his grandmother alert and aware made his day—hell, it made his week. He bent down and kissed her wrinkled cheek, his smile nearly as broad as hers.

"Hi granny, how are you doing?" He said while pulling up a nearby chair.

"Well other than it being hot enough to melt this fake costume jewelry, I'm fairing well."

He burst out laughing. He loved when his grandmother was like her old self. She was wearing big white plastic balls in her pierced ears and a matching bracelet and necklace. He didn't recognize it so it was probably a gift from one of the residents or staff.

"Helen," she said to a blue haired woman that was also sitting in a wheelchair right next to hers. "This is the grandson I've been telling you about." She turned to Riley. "Helen just got here a few days ago."

Helen leaned in and whispered loudly to Riley. "I've been here nearly a year, but your grandmother forgets things."

Grandma scowled. "All of us in here forget things or we wouldn't be here!" She calmed and reached out and patted Riley's beard. "Such a smart handsome boy."

His smile faded. Not so smart, and the handsome part was questionable. He thought about Stella for a split second and then he handed her one of the boxes.

"I brought you this."

She clapped her hands together. "Oh a gift!"

Once it was sitting in her lap he opened it and she exclaimed at the sight of the slice of pie.

"It's one of Miss Birdie's pies. There was a picnic at church today. She wanted me to bring you a slice."

"I love Birdie's pies." She looked at it lovingly. "There's so much. Can I share it with my friends?"

"You sure can. Let me find some more plates and forks." One of the attendants was standing nearby and she smiled at Riley. It was the older black lady that always spoke to him when no one else did. Next to her was a younger black woman that he didn't recognize.

"I'll bring out some plates." The older woman disappeared and returned a few moments later with plastic plates and forks. The younger woman had wordlessly walked away from him while he waited.

"Jasper," Granny called over to two men playing checkers. A thin black man looked up. "Come and try some of this pie that my grandson brought."

Jasper smiled. "Why that sounds mighty fine." He used a cane and ambled over. Riley peered at him in surprise. Did his grandma just call this man her friend?

"Hello there, young man." Jasper said while holding out his hand. He was dressed dapper in tan slacks, which had been ironed perfectly so that the crease was razor sharp. He had on black shoes that were shined bright enough to show your reflection, and a white button down shirt completed the ensemble.

Riley noticed a few of the black staff members watching him curiously. He shook Jasper's hand.

"Nice to meet you, sir." He said politely. One of the staff members cursed under her breath while another chuckled. When he saw them discreetly exchange money he hid a frown.

Riley ended up cutting both slices of pie and splitting it equally between himself, granny, Jasper and Helen. They ate their feast around a small table containing a potted plant, which Riley placed temporarily on the floor.

Granny was smacking her lips as she ate. "Birdie made the best lemon pie. I tried my damndest to get that recipe. I even had Vera down at the market spy on her for me, but I swear she sabotaged the ingredients. There's no way she used concentrated lemons and lemon JELLO." Granny narrowed her eyes suspiciously. "She was a sneak like that."

"It is a very good pie." Helen agreed.

"Best I've ever had." Jasper stated while smacking his lips.

"This always tasted so good with coffee." Granny replied.

"Hold that thought." Riley stood and went over to where the kindly attendant and the young black woman were once again standing, observing the residents.

"Can we get some coffee?" Riley asked.

"Certainly Mr. Pranger." The lady said with a smile that indicated that she didn't mind at all, even though it probably wasn't her job to go running after items for him.

"It will have to be decaf," the younger woman stated while eyeing him as if she didn't like what she saw.

"I doubt if they'll know the difference," he replied. The woman who was probably in her early thirties just looked at him.

"Please let us know in the future if you intend to bring sweets. Some of the residents take insulin." She said coldly. So she didn't like him. He almost told her that if her buddies hadn't been so busy taking bets on him then they could have mentioned it before he shared the pie.

But then he remembered what Stella had said last night—something to the effect that blacks (*Negroes*) didn't care what poor white trash thought of them. His cheeks flamed at the memory. Did this woman think that he looked down on her or on any person just because they were attendants? In her eyes was he nothing more than poor white trash?

The older attendant returned with a tray containing a pot of coffee, small coffee cups, packs of sugar, sweetener and cream.

"Thank you." Riley said where normally he would have muttered it.

After the pie and coffee they went inside to cool off in the lounge. Jasper and Helen came along and they all talked about music and television. After an hour he lightly gripped his grandmother's hand and kissed it. Why couldn't she be like this all the time?

"I need to get going, granny."

She reached up and gave him a hug. "Okay, sonny boy."

"Nice to meet you Miss Helen, Mr. Jasper." He shook hands with them and they thanked him for the pie.

"See you next week." He called over his shoulder as he left.

"Thanks for coming to visit," his grandmother replied with a smile that seemed to cover her entire face.

As he was leaving he saw the young black woman on the porch watching the other residents.

He almost walked right past her but then he stopped. "My grandmother's doing good today." He said with a smile. "I hope it lasts." The woman's expression shifted, the cool wariness retreated...a bit.

"I hope so too. There's no cure for Alzheimer's but with the right medication we can slow down its progression."

He nodded. "I just want her to be comfortable."

The woman hesitated. "It's good that you visit every week. A lot of the residents don't get visitors unless it's their birthday or Christmas. They get so lonely here." She looked him in the eyes. "Making friends is all they have sometimes."

"Then I'm happy she's made friends." He said. He tilted his head, curious that she knew so much about these people. "Aren't you a new attendant? I've never seen you before."

"I'm not an attendant. I'm a doctor," she said with an edge of disapproval at his assumption. "I generally visit during the week." Her expression changed as she studied him. "When she's having good days she has friends. But then there are days when she lives in the past. Those aren't always good days for any of us; friends or staff included." The doctor continued to stare at him.

"She can be cantankerous." Riley said softly thinking about how easily Sully had thrown around the N-word yesterday.

"Yes. Cantankerous." The doctor said while staring at him.

Riley nodded and then left.

Chapter Fourteen

"Do you think it's safe for them to be on the Pranger's property?" Ashleigh asked Christopher as they drove home with Stella and Adam following behind.

Christopher glanced at the rearview mirror and Ashleigh followed his line of sight to Brianna who was listening intently. Yeah, it was best to table this conversation.

When Stella pulled up to the large A-frame house she instantly fell in love with it. She and Ashleigh stood outside for a few moments talking about how it had been built as a near replica of one built by Christopher's uncle Ray.

"A lot of the homes are like that on the hill." Ashleigh explained. "Including the gingerbread house."

"Yes, Riley told me the story about how his dad and grandfather had built it for his grandparents."

Ashleigh was surprised that he'd revealed so much. She'd seen Riley often enough but had never seen him string together more than a few words.

"We'll show you around," Christopher said while holding his son on his hip. "Brianna, baby, you can show Adam around."

It was clear to Stella that Christopher truly loved his family. It wasn't long before she even forgot that Ashleigh and Christopher were different races. They went together so well.

She loved the house. Even though it was a new construction, every room felt quaint. She had the feeling of being in an old French villa, weird but true. The furniture and décor was stylish and modern but it still fit in perfectly with the hand hued wooden floors and old-fashioned character.

Chris Jr. had fallen asleep so Christopher left the women to themselves while he put him down for his nap. He was happy that Ashleigh had something new to take her mind off things. With Kendra and Lance back in Cincinnati she tended to keep things bottled in. He knew that she was depressed but wouldn't admit it, especially not to him. It was because she didn't want him to stop going on the missions, knowing that they were more than just his job—besides his family it was the most important part of his life. He had one coming at the end of summer and when he told her he had seen the way her eyes had changed, the way she was mentally preparing for him to die.

He couldn't explain to her that he wouldn't allow himself to die, not when he finally had all of the things that he could have ever wished for. She didn't understand what happened to him during the Special Missions. He was a machine— no, he was the Beast that they all knew him to be. He was ruthless, because he couldn't afford to be anything less. There was blood on his hands— buckets of it but when he looked into the eyes of those that loved him it was all worth it.

"Grandma," Brianna said to the older woman who was in the kitchen preparing lunch.

"Yes, baby?" She saw Adam. "Who's your friend?"

"This is Adam. He's going to be up here for the summer."

"Oh that's nice."

"Grandma, can we make some ice cream? Adam never had it homemade before."

"Oh that's a good idea." The older woman turned to Adam.

"Adam, what's your favorite flavor?"

"Chocolate." He said shyly.

"Then chocolate it is."

They were making the base when Ashleigh and Stella came in. Stella noticed that Ashleigh called her mother-in-law Mom and she wondered what it would be like if she had a traditional family with a husband and in-laws. Maybe she should try in earnest to be in a relationship. At the rate things were going, it appeared that was the only way that Adam would have a father in his life.

While the ice cream went into the freezer Brianna took Adam out back to the tree house that her daddy and uncle Butch had built.

"Wow!" He exclaimed, his eyes growing big. He'd never seen a real life tree house before. There was a rope ladder as well as planks nailed to the tree that you could use to climb.

Once inside he saw that it was decorated with a lot of pink things but he didn't mind. There were beanbag chairs, and books and even a dollhouse. He saw the string of lights running the circumference of the room and scratched his head.

"You have lights?" He asked.

"Yes. There's electricity." She pulled out a box fan from a crate and plugged it into the wall. "It gets hot up here."

"You can play video games up here...well if you had a television."

"I use my IPad here all the time." Adam suddenly wished that he had a tree house. But they lived in the suburbs so there was no way that he could ask for one of his own.

For the next half an hour they talked about everything from their favorite games, the latest Marvel Super hero movie, their best friends, and even about school and teachers. Very quickly they got to know each other, becoming fast friends.

"Where's your dad?" Brianna asked.

"I don't have one." Adam replied. He thought about Brianna's dad and how nice he seemed. There were days when he wished that he had a father like other kids, but for the most part his mother filled in all the blanks for him.

Brianna gave him a long look, as if she had questions but was too polite to ask. The silence dragged out a bit.

"I have two mothers," he finally said.

Brianna's eyes lit up. "Oh! That's like one of my best friends. He has two dads; my uncle Lance and uncle Rick."

Adam shook his head. "Not like that. I'm adopted. There's my birth mother and then my real mother."

"Your real mother?"

Adam nodded. He didn't talk about it much. His best friends knew but now that Brianna was one of his best friends he figured it was okay to tell her.

"Well my birth mother had me, but my real mother raises me. And she loves me."

Brianna smiled. "Yeah. Chad is adopted too. So he doesn't have a mother either—other than a birth mother, and I guess a birth father. So really he has one mom and three dads."

Adam smiled at that, but no, it didn't work like that. He explained that when you are put up for adoption those birth parents are no longer your mom and dad, the people that raise you are.

"That makes sense. But don't you think about who they are?"

He thought about lying but friends shouldn't lie. "Yeah. But I can find out when I turn eighteen. My birth mother has a letter for me. My mom told me about it."

"What's in the letter? I would go crazy wondering." Brianna said, her grey eyes going bright at the prospect of Princess's and millionaires.

"My mom already told me what's in it. It's basically her name and how to locate her—if I ever want to know that."

"Do you want to know?"

Adam shrugged. He truly wasn't sure. He just hoped that she would keep her distance.

Stella, Ashleigh, Christopher and his mother sat out on the sun porch. There was a large ceiling fan that kept them relatively cool and Mrs. Jameson, Christopher's mother, had brought out a pitcher of fresh squeezed lemonade. Stella confessed that it was the best lemonade she'd ever had. And with a proud smile Mrs. Jameson revealed that it was sweetened with honey instead of sugar.

"What brings you to vacation on Cobb Hill?" Christopher asked while getting relaxed in his chair.

"I read an article about the ginger bread house once and I always thought about taking Adam to the country. This was pretty close considering that we don't have any family down south."

Christopher noted that Stella averted her eyes frequently while giving her explanation. But at other times during the conversation she had looked at them squarely, even inquisitively. She was lying. But it didn't matter that much to him. Maybe she thought that it just wasn't any of his business, which it wasn't.

It's really pretty here." Ashleigh stated. "But the true appeal is the simplicity of life here in Cobb Hill. Our kids can run around and be loud without worrying about the neighbors hearing everything they do."

"It smells good, too." Stella said. She had noticed that right away. "I mean the air smells sweet. Even that water coming out of the spring is the best water I've ever had. And everyone is very nice..." she shrugged, "with the exception of Riley's cousin."

She relaxed against her chair and Christopher thought that she seemed to be thinking hard.

"You all know Riley—better than me." Stella finally said. "What kind of a man is he?" She looked away for a moment, staring out at the tree house where Adam and Brianna were playing. "I need to make sure that Adam's in a safe place."

Christopher leaned forward. "Did Adam hear any of the filth spewing from Sully? Because he and I have something of an agreement. If my children witness any of his stupidity I stomp him into the ground. I'm extending that to any child. If his bigotry is extended into bullying children I will have to hurt him." Christopher practically growled this statement out.

Stella believed every word. She didn't get the sense that he was some tough guy, but he was a protector. His wife rubbed his white knuckles because his fists were balled tight.

"He'll do it too." Christopher's mother stated. "And Sully will deserve every bit of it. He's very bad news. You stay away from that one. Riley's not a bad guy, but Sully is."

"Thankfully Adam didn't hear anything too bad." Stella stated.

Ashleigh leaned forward. "I don't like gossiping and spreading rumors. But you do have your son on that property so I'll tell you what I know. Sully killed a man a few years back."

Stella's mouth parted while her heart pounded in her chest. She finally let out a long breath.

Ashleigh continued. "He went to jail and got out a short time later because he claimed self defense. And in truth, it might have been. Both were pretty bad news."

"Oh my God..." Stella said with a shaky voice. She hadn't considered that she had been in the vicinity of a criminal that had taken another man's life. She suddenly felt cold. She looked over at where Adam was playing and chills ran over her skin.

Being in the Pranger family wouldn't be a good choice for Adam. Racists and murderers...She'd had all the best intentions of telling Riley that he was Adam's biological father, but there was a reason that Adam's birth mother hadn't told him. Maybe she needed to keep it that way...

Christopher's mother was watching the emotions that played across Stella's face. There was more there than the young woman had revealed. She didn't know what it was about but there was something.

"Stella," she said. "You could judge Riley by his family but it wouldn't be fair. In my family we have bootleggers, and philanderers and even some wannabe Klans people. I wouldn't want anybody to judge me on them.

"Riley's never gotten into trouble and he's a good person. He goes to church every Sunday, he visits his grandmother once a week and when everyone else took off he was the one to take care of her. I like Riley. I can't say that about any other Pranger including his mama and daddy. But somehow he turned out better than any of them."

Christopher shrugged. "He ain't all good. Bodie fired him for some reason, mama. And if Bodie fired him than there's a good reason for it."

Ashleigh was shaking her head. "Nobody knows the real reason he got fired."

"So Riley doesn't have a job?" Stella interrupted.

"He just got fired about a week ago," Ashleigh replied. "Before that he'd been working for the last four or five years at a garage owned by Bodie. If Riley was a redneck than there's no way that Bodie Matthews would have ever let him within a foot of Shaun and the girls." Christopher conceded to that point with a nod. Ashleigh continued. "Bodie is white and Shaun's black. So you see, he's the best judge of character. He's worked with him up close for years."

"Until he fired him a week ago. Blood's been bad between them every since." Christopher had heard the rumors just like everybody else.

"There's a lot of speculation about the reason," Mrs. Jameson took over the story. "But one of the other employees was undocumented and got deported. Rumor has it that Riley said something to that no-good cousin of his who then informed the authorities. The rest is known by only Riley and Bodie."

"He got fired over something that someone else might have done?" Stella asked incredulously.

"I know, right?" Ashleigh said.

"We don't know the reason. But Bodie is one of the most level headed men that I know." Christopher wasn't sure what to think but he was inclined to side with Bodie over Riley. "If he let him go after Pete got deported than he must have had a good reason."

Stella listened quietly to their conversation as it went back and forth from person to person. Christopher just didn't like the Prangers at all while Mrs. Jameson and Ashleigh seemed to see Riley in a different light. She could understand that. No one should be judged on anything other than his or her own merit.

Telling Riley about Adam was too important for her to dismiss him so quickly. She would have to put more thought into it.

Chapter Fifteen

They sat down to a lunch of tomato soup and sandwiches. Mrs. Jameson apologized that it wasn't anything special but Stella told her that it was indeed special because it meant that she didn't have to prepare lunch.

Adam watched Brianna's dad load his sandwich with ham, roast beef, and turkey. And then he added slices of tomato, lettuce, onions, mustard *and* mayo. He mimicked him and his mother warned that he had better eat all that he put on his plate. Adam assured her that he would but she ended up splitting half of the sandwich with him and then having some soup.

When the baby woke up Christopher put him in his high chair and they laughed at the mess that he made with his little cup of soup and crackers.

Brianna was a chatterbox and once they discovered that Adam was learning Japanese he was persuaded to share some words and phrases with them.

There was a great deal to talk about, especially since both families lived in Cincinnati.

They finished up lunch by enjoying the homemade ice cream and both women were pretty sure that they had made a new friend. It was hard to tell over just one visit, but Stella liked the petite woman with eyes that softened whenever they settled on her husband and kids. And Ashleigh really liked the way Stella carried herself so eloquently. Stella was naturally beautiful without a face full of makeup, and she was stylish in a low-key manner. Her height and weight seemed to be an asset—something that she wish she had learned back when she had struggled with her weight.

Brianna didn't want Adam to leave. Ashleigh and Christopher had made them promise to come back to visit soon and Stella said she would. She meant it too. Ashleigh explained that no matter how nice it was on Cobb Hill, kids still needed other kids to play with and Christopher Jr. just wasn't old enough to keep his sister's attention— at least once he got tired of playing dress up with her.

As Stella and Adam drove back to the gingerbread cottage he yawned tiredly.

"Are you ready for a nap?" Stella asked pleased that for two days in a row she'd found things to keep her son occupied.

"I'm too big to take naps." He replied.

"Well I could use a nap and I'm much bigger than you."

He just grinned but before they reached the cottage he was fast asleep.

"You're getting too big for this," she said to herself while lifting him up and out of his seat. But then he wrapped his arms around her neck and snuggled against her shoulder and she smiled. Nope, never too old for this.

Riley looked out the window when he heard the SUV drive up. He had wondered where his boarders were, but was pleased to know that they hadn't just been cooped up inside the cottage all day.

He saw Stella carrying the boy and it caused him to smile. He was a big boy but she didn't look like she had any trouble managing his weight. Where was his father? She hadn't mentioned it the day before. He blew out a long breath at the memory of how disastrous their evening had turned out. He was ashamed at how it had turned out.

He returned to his meal. It was delicious, as usual. But he didn't enjoy it. He chewed while staring at nothing in particular.

After cleaning up the dishes and pacing for a few minutes he got up the nerves to go over to the cottage and to apologize again. After mulling over it for the last few hours he realized that his last apology had been weak and he'd come off as defensive.

When he was standing on the porch of the cottage he abruptly stopped, turned and started walking back to the main house.

This was stupid! He turned again and headed back to the cottage. Then he knocked before he could chicken out.

When Stella answered the door he saw that her hair was wrapped in a colorful silk scarf and that she was wearing shorts and a t-shirt with socks on her feet.

He realized with a blush that he'd taken all of that in before even speaking.

"Hey." He finally said.

"Hey," she said. Now that she'd discovered so much more about Riley she looked at him with a new appreciation—although it was hard not to appreciate his big toned torso in a faded t-shirt and worn jeans that seemed to hug his legs and butt perfectly. "Come in." She stepped aside and he walked into the room.

"I hope I wasn't interrupting." He asked.

"No. It's fine. I wanted to talk to you…about last night."

He bit his lip. "Me too." He looked around. "Where's Adam?"

"Napping." She gestured for him to come into the front room and to sit. She sat on the loveseat, folding her long legs beneath her. He noted that her legs took up the entire seat whereas the average woman would have just taken up a corner.

She was so graceful, he thought. She was probably the tallest woman that he'd ever met but she carried herself as if she was petite and as delicate as a piece of china.

He sat down in one of the armchairs, remembering how hard it had been for his grandparents to afford the monthly payments for the furniture. Paying it off was like how it was for some people to make their last payment on a car loan. He sat gingerly as if his grandmother was about to round the corner and reprimand him for allowing his jeans on the fabric.

"We went on a hike and then met the Jamesons and had lunch with them." Stella said.

"Yeah the Jamesons are the family I was telling Adam about yesterday--the one with the little girl his age. I didn't think he was much interested at the time....little girls and all."

Stella smiled. "Well they hit it off."

"That's good." There was a pause and Riley cleared his throat.

"You don't have to apologize for what happened yesterday," she interrupted. "I know that I came off rude to you. But it really wasn't anything that you did wrong. I was still angry. But at him, not you."

"I feel really bad about what happened," he said.

"I know Riley. But..." she paused.

"What?"

"It's just that your cousin-"

"I set him straight. He will not give you or Adam any more problems. I promise."

She blew out a relieved breath. "Can you..."

"What?" He asked.

"Can you keep him off the property while we're here? I know it's a lot to ask—" she looked him square in the eye. "I heard about the trouble he got into."

Riley nodded right away. "Under the circumstances I think your request is warranted.

He won't be around here as long as you or Adam are here. Okay?"

She finally smiled. "Okay."

"Did my cousin say…say anything to Adam?" If he did then he'd let Sully have it for sure.

"No. I sent Adam back to the house once he implied that Adam was a mistake because he's mixed race."

Riley gnawed his lip, his face felt like the color was draining from it as his anger began to once again rise.

"I sent Adam back to the cottage once I realized where the conversation was going. And that's when you came out. Later I talked to him about it but he didn't understand any of it."

"Okay." Riley said shortly. "Thanks for telling me. I'm sorry I left you with him even for the short time that I did. I realized when I got back that he'd just sent me on a wild goose chase just so that he could do his dirt. If I thought he'd do something like that I swear to you that I would have never left like that."

She was utterly surprised at his confession. Riley Pranger was just like her, straight to the point, no chaser. It was a rare thing to see in a man.

"I believe you," she said. "I can't be mad at you. I saw the shock on your face. I don't blame you for any of it."

He stood, feeling a weight lift from his shoulders. "I better get going." He headed for the front door. "If you need anything just let me know." She followed him.

"Riley?"

He turned and looked at her. "Yeah?"

"What happened to your leg? I noticed you limping. It's worse today."

He looked down at his knee. "Playing college ball. I took a bad hit. It still hurts sometimes." He looked suddenly uncomfortable.

"I'm sorry for being nosey."

"No, you're fine. It's just that I had a promising career...and now I don't."

She nodded. "I'm sorry."

"I'm over it." He shrugged. "Let me know if you need anything." He turned and left. She watched him for a few moments and realized that she felt sorry for him. He was a nice man, a little sad, a little lonely. Yes. She would tell him about Adam. She didn't hold any expectations whatsoever. But she would tell him for better or for worse.

Chapter Sixteen

On Monday morning Riley got a phone call from Mr. Harper at the hardware store. He wanted to know if Riley would be okay taking part-time hours and of course Riley said yes. Anything was better than nothing.

When he told Riley the hourly pay, his heart sank. It was better than minimum wage but not by much.

"When can I start?" He asked, being sure to sound enthusiastic.

"Today if you want."

"Today is fine."

"Okay. Be here by about noon and we'll get your paperwork completed and start training you."

"Okay Mr. Harper. And thank you."

"You're welcome, Riley. You're a hard worker. Some of these kids around here don't know the meaning of the word. You fixed my truck that one time and even washed it for me. I always appreciated that."

Riley remembered that. He didn't normally wash the vehicles but he remembered that there was road salt on it and it had been pushing summer.

After he hung up with Mr. Harper Riley smiled in relief, then he whooped and hurried up the stairs to shower and prepare for the day.

He arrived a bit before noon so he decided to head over to the grocery store and pick up a few items. Mrs. Lemon was working and she greeted him with a broad smile.

"Hiya Riley. Congratulations on your new job."

His mouth was opened and prepared to greet her before her revelation left him stunned and mute.

"Uh...yeah. I was just getting ready to head on over there." He said in surprise. Why was he surprised that his business had spread so fast? She probably knew about the job even before he did.

His suspicions were confirmed when she came over and winked at him. "I know Chase Harper. I put a bug in his ear that you were a good fella and that he should give you a chance. He's going to be starting you off pretty small but hang in there Riley. He needs a good manager and he can't trust them teenagers that just want to run willy nilly around town."

Riley smiled at her and before he could stop himself he gave her a hug. "Thank you Miss Lemon. I appreciate you."

She blushed and looked very pleased but he quickly released her and with a blush of his own he grabbed a bag of chips and a pint of lemonade. He quickly paid and hurried out of the store eating his purchase and checking his phone for the time. He had about five minutes, time enough to finish up his snack and be at the hardware store promptly at 11:59.

Stella stood at the entrance of the loft watching Adam playing one of his video games. He was still wearing pajamas even though it was after twelve.

They had both been pretty tired and had slept in late this morning. She had spent the latter part of the morning using her cell phone to take care of some business. She then updated her social media — noted that Evan had commented on some of her posts. She ignored him. She then chatted for a few minutes with her mom. But now she wanted to do something that didn't entail being inside the cottage.

"What should we do today?"

Adam shrugged, his concentration more on his game than on her.

"We can go fishing." She suggested.

Now she got his full attention. He paused the game. "Yeah, that would be cool."

She smiled and turned to leave. "Go and get ready. We need to buy some fishing poles."

When they left the cottage, Stella noted that Riley's truck was gone and she wondered briefly how he spent his time since he was unemployed.

She decided to stick to the mountain because frankly going up and down that mountainside three days in a row was too much for her nerves. She remembered the little hardware store across the street from the market that they'd visited the day before, and headed for it.

"What are we going to do if we actually catch some fish?" Adam asked as they parked and entered the store.

"We'll eat them—and not *if* but *when* we catch them."

Riley was being shown how to work the cash register by his 'supervisor' a teen on summer break from high school, when he heard Adam's voice.

"Mom, it's Riley. Hi Riley!" He came rushing over to the counter and Riley looked at him in surprise. He found himself smiling at the boy's enthusiasm at seeing him.

"Hi, Adam." Suddenly he looked around for Stella who was just rounding the corner carrying two fishing poles. She had an equally surprised look on her face at the sight of him behind the counter wearing a nametag pinned to his shirt with 'Riley' written in black magic marker.

"Riley," she said. "I didn't know you..." she nearly said 'had a job' but even saying 'work here' didn't seem appropriate. She thrust the two fishing poles toward him.

A young teen that was popping sweet smelling bubble gum accepted the poles. "I'll take those." He said. "He can't use the cash register yet."

Riley's face warmed, but he looked at the poles. "Gonna do some fishing, huh?"

"Yeah," Adam replied. "We saw a lake with fish in it."

"We sell fishing licenses." The cashier said after blowing a loud bubble.

"Fishing license?" Stella asked.

"Yes ma'am. You need a license to fish in Estill County."

Riley rolled his eyes and took the poles from the cashier and handed them back to Stella. "Go put these back. I got plenty of poles at the house."

He gave the teen a sideways look. "And I knew plenty of private lakes where you can fish for free."

The cashier scowled. "Uh...Riley can I speak to you?" He hissed.

"I'll be back," he said to Stella and Adam before following his supervisor to the back.

"Riley," the teen said. "You just lost us a sale. You never dissuade our customers not to purchase our products. Sales are going to be part of your commission. Also, if you happen to have friends that come into the store, please try to maintain a professional manner."

"Uh...I didn't realize that I wasn't interacting professionally." Riley said.

"Well you were holding a conversation with them." His supervisor popped his gum as if it was an exclamation point to his final words.

Riley just nodded his head. "Gotcha."

When they returned to the storefront, Stella and Adam had returned the fishing poles and were waiting at the counter.

Ignoring his supervisor Riley leaned against the counter. "When were you two planning on fishing?"

"Just whenever," Stella shrugged.

"Will you go fishing with us?" Adam asked.

Stella nodded. "You're gonna show us where we can fish for free, anyways."

The teen cleared his throat. Riley ignored him. "The best fishing is done in the mornings. How about tomorrow?" His work schedule looked pretty sparse with him mostly working the weekends and evenings.

Stella looked at the teen who was now tapping on the counter as if he was perturbed. "We can talk about it later. Come on, lets go Adam."

Adam held up a package of batteries. "Can we get these?"

"Yep," She slid them across the counter at the kid who punched up the sale in satisfaction.

Riley found himself whistling as he drove home from work. He'd only worked until six — not a full day's work but he wasn't complaining. He pulled his truck behind Stella's and instead of going to his house he headed over to the cottage.

Adam opened the door for him. "Hi Riley. Come in. Mom's in the kitchen."

"Hey Adam." He stepped inside surprised at the sound of the music playing softly from a blue tooth speaker. It was a mellow R&B crooner and Riley was willing to bet that it was the first time R&B music had ever been played within the walls of this cottage.

Stella stepped out of the kitchen to greet him. "We were just getting read to eat dinner. It's just spaghetti and sauce that I made with the leftover hamburger from yesterday if you'd care to join us."

It did smell good and he was hungry. Also, one thing that he had noticed about Stella is that she if she offered an invitation it didn't just seem to be an obligatory offer. He could tell that she wanted him to accept it.

"Thanks. I did skip lunch."

Adam also seemed happy that he accepted the offer.

"What do you want to drink?" Stella asked as she peered into the refrigerator. "Bottled water, iced tea or wine? I'm having wine."

"Iced tea is fine." He replied. Adam was showing him the characters that he had created on his Gameboy system.

"I played on one of these when I was a kid. I don't remember it being able to do all this," he replied in interest as he accepted Adam's invitation to create an avatar in his likeness. He'd always been interested in video games but obviously with his family's income it was something they could never afford. Sometimes he went to a school friend's house and played on their systems, which gave him his limited understanding of such things.

"Alright, boys. It's time to eat." Stella said as she placed the salad on the table.

Riley took a seat and suddenly he had a strange sense of nostalgia—only twisted up because instead of the white faces of his grandparents, and the backdrop of the evening news droning in the background, there was the faces of two African American's and the backdrop of a Kanye West tune playing in the background. The funny thing is that both gave him an equal sense of comfort.

Chapter Seventeen

When they piled into Riley's truck at exactly six am the next morning, Stella was surprised at all the things Riley had brought just to go fishing. Yes, of course there were the poles, even the extra poles were understandable. And yes, of course they needed the tackle box—she hadn't considered it yesterday. But he also had a bucket, which was to hold the fish they caught. He had an old margarine bowl filled with worms. Its lid was tightly in place but it had small slits in top to allow air. He explained that his preferred bait was wax-worms but corn was also fine so he had also brought along an ear of corn.

In the back of the truck were folding chairs, and a cooler, which Stella had filled with bottled water, soda and sandwiches.

As Riley pulled out of the driveway, Stella realized something. This was the first time that she and Adam had spent time alone with a man not related to them. Riley was the first man that she'd allowed around her son, and she was surprised to see that Adam seemed to enjoy the experience.

She peered at them as they discussed the different types of fish they might catch.

"Blue gill is the most common in these parts. But I've caught trout and there's always catfish."

"Which is the best?" Adam asked.

"Trout is good and it's big. But I like blue gill. They're smaller and their bones are harder to get at but if you know what you're doing you can slide the bones right out. The meat is real sweet and flaky. My mama sure knew how to fry up some fish."

"Did she teach you how to fry fish?" Adam asked.

"Yep. I'll fry us up a batch."

"If we catch some." Adam replied.

"Nah, we'll catch some."

Stella listened to them and with a jolt she realized that she felt comfortable. Driving through the mountains with the first blush of sun rising in the horizon, listening to Riley and Adam chitchatting, it dawned on her that she had never felt this way because she had never opened herself up to allow a man to give her this feeling.

Maybe...maybe she could warm up to the idea of letting someone into her life. She peeked at Riley who briefly met her look. Their eyes locked for just a split second and in that moment Stella didn't feel as if she was with a stranger. In that moment looking into grey eyes that were familiar to her because they were nearly the exact eyes that she looked into each day when she looked at the face of her child, made her feel as if everything was in it's right place.

Riley drove confidently through the narrow roads taking a turn off into a nearly hidden path that made Stella grip her armrest. How in the hell had he even seen this turn off? But she trusted that he knew what he was doing. Also the sun had risen so she could at least see what was in front of them.

A short time later they reached a small lake. Flat rocks surrounded it and it was obvious that although in an obscure location it had been used by others, evidence by a small weathered pier.

They carried their items to a spot at the lake's edge and not onto the pier.

"No shade there. When the sun comes up it's going to get blistering hot." Riley explained when Adam asked.

Stella set up the chairs and Riley tried not to watch, he tried to be casual. But in the truck there had been something—he'd felt it like an electrical jolt. She'd looked at him and it was as if a current had passed between them. He couldn't deny that he liked them both but was he ready to *like* someone again? It had been years since Jasmine...plus where was Adam's father? How did a schoolteacher and single mother afford to drop a grand for a month in a country cottage and afford to drive a Lexus?

Before the day ended he intended to find out the answer. In the meantime he just wanted to enjoy himself and to relive the joy of fishing by teaching Adam. It had been something that he'd loved doing with his father and grandfather. Even when they did it because they needed meat to add to the dinner pot, it had been something that had given him a sense of peace. He supposed because fishing allowed him isolation from everything else, and during those times he could forget the ugliness that he so often saw.

Riley got their fishing poles prepared. He even had a smaller one just perfect for Adam. Stella noted how patient he was when he taught Adam to bait his hook and the best way to cast. She was then very grateful that he was here because she had no idea half of what it took to fish.

He offered to put a worm on her hook but she puffed out her chest.

"Nope. I can do it." But when the guts began to ooze out she squealed and dropped the reel and did a tap dance that lasted several seconds. "It got on my hand!" She cried while shaking it out in front of her.

"Mom!" Adam hissed. "You're going to scare away the fish." He placed his reel neatly to the ground and then dug a tissue out of his pocket and grabbed her hand. He wiped it carefully. "There."

Riley tried not to smile at the look of shame on Stella's face. Riley grabbed the corn and handed it to her.

"Thanks." She said quietly. She caught the look of amusement that Riley was trying to hide and ignored it. She was prepared to be the first one to catch a fish and she wouldn't squeal once, even when she had to take it off the hook.

They sat in their chairs and relaxed. Even Adam appeared to appreciate the quiet, and didn't seem to miss his Gameboy.

Stella found herself peeking at Riley, appreciating his long legs in worn jeans and the way his muscles moved whenever he cast or reeled. And Riley made every effort not to keep looking at Stella. She wore jeans with holes strategically place along her knees and thighs. She also wore a simple shirt that looked old but he thought that she wore it too well for it to be anything less than designer.

Today her hair was once again pulled up but instead of an Afro puffball it was a silky ponytail that nearly touched her shoulder blades. It was a hair weave or hairpiece but he liked it. He couldn't always say that he liked the wigs and weaves that the girls wore down in Eastern University. Sometimes they had been just ridiculously fake looking. Stella's at least looked real, and he might not have ever known the difference if he hadn't seen her wearing the other one.

Adam caught the first fish half an hour after they arrived. He called it small but Riley told him that it was just right for a blue gill.

"I can eat three of these." Adam complained.

"Well you better get back to fishing if we're going to catch enough to fill us all up."

Riley placed the fish on a string and set it back in the water. Within the hour there were four more fish to join it. When Stella caught her first fish she bravely removed the hook from it's mouth but couldn't bring herself to place it on the string. It seemed Barbaric. She asked if they could just put them out of their misery and filet them now. Riley explained that they would start going bad. But he didn't make fun of her for asking and she appreciated that.

"So you're a school teacher." Riley finally stated. "I might have taken that up while in college if I thought I'd be able to drive a Lexus."

While Stella normally didn't like when men wanted to know something but were too polite to just come out and ask, but she thought Riley's method of asking about her finances was pretty cute. Besides, he was the father of her son. He had a right to know.

"The rumors are true that school teachers don't make all that much. I've been lucky."

He nodded. It seemed so.

Stella crossed one of her long legs. "When I was a teenager, I read that the typical millionaire has at least six streams of revenue." Her eyes locked onto his and her expression became serious. "I have three...for now.

"I invested in an up and coming wig company while I was in college." She'd used part of her college loans to do it and by the time that she'd graduated she had earned enough to pay them off in one year.

The company made wigs and hair weaves for black women to purchase online. Now purchasing hair online was common but the company that she had partnered with had been one of the trendsetters.

She made more money with her investments than she made as a teacher but she didn't get the same joy. Plus, if she hadn't been a teacher she would have never met Adam.

Riley's eyes moved up to her hair. "I definitely took the wrong career path." He joked.

"I think you had different plans," Stella said.

Riley nodded and then looked out at the lake.

When it was close to nine am they decided to leave. Adam, of course wanted to stay longer but he was beginning to get sunburned and Stella hadn't brought any sunscreen.

"We have enough fish for a proper fish fry." Riley announced as he transferred the fish to the bucket and placed it in the back of the truck. They had caught nine and for the three of them it would be plenty.

"Are you going to clean them?" Adam asked Riley, while trying not to look at his mother. Stella opened her mouth to offer but couldn't bring herself to say the words.

"Yep. You gonna help me?" He asked the young boy.

Adam nodded enthusiastically.

"Do you have to work today?" Stella asked him.

"Yeah but not until six." He would be closing for the rest of the week and then doing stock, which was fine with him. His teenybopper supervisor seemed to think that being a cashier was a privilege.

"When we get home Adam and I'll get the fish cleaned up. Then we can meet in the back yard at about...lets say eleven, and I'll get the deep fryer going."

"Sounds like a plan. I'll make something to go with the fish." Stella said.

"French fries," Adam said.

"French fries it is," Stella agreed.

Once home they unloaded the truck. Adam and Riley headed for the backyard to clean the fish and Stella decided that she would just watch from a far. She didn't think that she was ready to leave Adam and Riley alone but once she saw the blood and guts appear on the newspaper clad picnic table, she decided that she would go back to the cottage and get a bath. Yes. Tonight had to be the night that she told Riley about Adam. After seeing them together it was no longer a question.

She ran a hot bath and as she soaked she felt the nervous knots build in her stomach at the prospect of telling Riley about having a son. She was afraid, maybe even a little guilty. She wasn't afraid that Riley could take Adam from her. She had already made sure that he couldn't legally gain custody of him. But the idea that she'd known that this man had a child out in the world and she'd sat on that information felt wrong. Even though she knew that it was in her and Adam's best interest to check him out first, she still felt bad. It wasn't just that. She also felt bad that she'd kept Adam away from his father. Seeing them together over the last few days proved that he could benefit from having his father in his life.

Stella was a firm believer that having a dick didn't make one a father. People said that it took a man to raise a man. As a single mother she had always fought that idea. She knew that there were plenty of men out there that made babies but were in no way father material. How did knocking up a woman make you equipped to be a good parent?

She knew she was both a good mother *and* father to her son. And for anyone to have the nerves to even suggest that a man could do a better job just might cause her to flip out. She was raising Adam to be the man that would thrive in this world. She was equipping him with knowledge and skills, while reinforcing his sense of self-worth and she would be damned if some idiot was going to suggest that she couldn't be successful at it because she didn't have a dick.

But after seeing Adam and Riley together a new idea began to surface. There actually was something that she couldn't give Adam, and it had nothing to do with her sex, her skills, her love, or her dedication to her child. What she couldn't give Adam was simply a second perspective.

Stella got out of the tub just when Adam returned home. She got his bath prepared as he went on and on about Riley, fishing, and how gross the fish guts were but that he hadn't been afraid.

"Mom. Do you think it would be okay if I watched sports with Riley sometime?"

She lathered his washcloth. "You'll have to ask him about that. But I don't want you to bother him too much, okay? He's been nice but we don't want to be pests."

"Okay," Adam said, his body seeming to deflate.

Stella washed his armpits but he didn't giggle like he normally did. "You like Riley?"

"Yeah."

"That's good. I'll talk to him about it, okay? Right after we eat. You can come back here and maybe play a video game or something while I talk to him about it."

Adam smiled suddenly. "Okay."

She took in a deep breath. There was no backing out now.

Chapter Eighteen

Riley had to run to the store for more oil for the deep fryer and while he was there he saw Theresa, Pete's woman coming out of the post office. She was giggling with some guy that he didn't recognize.

Hmph. She seemed pretty happy for someone whose husband was in lockup preparing to get deported. When she saw him, her face instantly changed, her expression becoming a shade angry but also a shade guilty. She snatched her hand away from the guy who had been holding it.

The guy tried to place his arm around her waist and she slapped it away and muttered something to him. Riley scowled and loaded his purchase into his truck. The guy was young, maybe even still in high school but Riley knew when two people were messing around. Theresa, Pete's wife was fucking that guy.

Once home, Riley had enough time to get a quick shower and then went down to the kitchen to whip up a batch of seasoned cornmeal using his mama's special recipe. Stella and Adam arrived while the oil was getting hot.

He hadn't meant to stare at her but he couldn't help it. She was just wearing simple capris pants but that blouse...wow. It was shaped like two handkerchiefs with points that fell to her waist. When she moved the wispy material flowed around her hips and he got a peek of her brown belly and her tiny bellybutton.

Her hair was down in a bob that surrounded her face. This hair was different, but it had to be her real hair. Regardless, he thought it was lovely. She wore pale lip-gloss on her full lips but he couldn't tell if she wore any other makeup, she just looked natural and fresh. Wow, was all he could think.

She was carrying a paper sack and he assumed that it contained the potatoes.

"I'm hungry." Adam proclaimed. "Can I have one of those apples?" he asked.

"Yep. They're in the kitchen on the counter."

Adam sprinted towards the house.

"Come right back out, Adam!" Stella called. He waved his hand at her without turning.

Riley watched him. "He's a good kid. His father isn't part of his life?"

Stella gave him a wry smile. She took a deep breath and then her mouth closed and she chickened out.

"Sorry for being nosey," Riley said quickly.

"No, you're fine." Stella said. "Adam doesn't know his father. But...I guess I'm hoping to change that."

Riley felt a sinking sensation. He wasn't sure what he had been thinking even to imagine that Stella might be interested in him. He was just a redneck living on a mountain in Kentucky. How was that supposed to work out, anyway? He wasn't one for one-night stands and...whatever. It wasn't going to happen so no use even thinking about any of that.

"I hope that works out." He said when Adam returned with his apple.

The fish and potatoes turned out to be an excellent fish fry. They ate every bit of it. And when Riley began to get too comfortable with Stella and Adam he remembered that Stella wanted to make it work with her son's father. The kid deserved it.

"I'm going to head on in and take a nap before work." He said while gathering the paper plates and napkins.

Adam looked at his mother quickly and mouthed something to her. She nodded.

Adam gave Riley a pleased look. "Thanks for taking us fishing. Bye!" Then he darted back to the cottage.

Riley smiled in confusion. "Okay..."

Stella was standing there wringing her fingers. He gave her a curious look. She looked nervous. He'd seen her laugh, he'd seen her pissed, and he had even seen her apologetic but seeing her nervous seemed wrong.

"Everything okay?" He asked.

"Riley…Can we sit down for a minute?"

"Yeah." He sat back down at the picnic table. She sat down across from him and then crossed her hands on the tabletop.

"Riley. I didn't come up to Cobb Hill just to vacation." His brow gathered as he waited for her to continue. "I came up to meet you."

He gave her an inquisitive look. "You came up to meet me? Why?"

"Because I felt that you needed to know something. It was something that I didn't think I could tell you by letter or over the phone. And truthfully, it was something that I had to tell you only after I got to know who you were. Now that I've met you…"

He frowned and shrugged. "Stella, what are you talking about?"

"I came here to tell you that Adam is your son." She waited for him to react so that she would know what to say next.

He just stared at her as if waiting for the punch line. Finally he asked. "What?" What in the hell was she talking about? Adam was his son? He'd never seen this woman before. And if he'd had sex with a six-foot tall black woman as gorgeous as her he surely wouldn't have forgotten it.

Was she trying to trick him into something crazy? It wasn't like he was rich and she could hit him up for money. What was this crazy shit? Was she a nutcase?

"When you were in college you dated a woman named Jasmine Chambers," she continued.

"Yeah...so?"

"A black woman."

"What does her race have anything to do with-?"

"Jasmine got pregnant, had a baby and placed that baby up for adoption. I adopted that baby. His name is Adam. And I came up on this mountain to meet you and to tell you that you are Adam's biological father."

Riley stared at her for so long that Stella wondered if he hadn't lost it.

Riley suddenly couldn't breath. "Stella." He finally spoke. "What are you telling me? Are you telling me that I have a kid?" He stood up before she could reply. He paced in one direction while holding his palms against his head. And then he stopped and paced in the opposite direction. He stopped long enough to look at Stella with wide, searching eyes before beginning the process of pacing all over again.

"Jasmine." He suddenly stopped and looked at Stella again. "Why would she do that? Why would she fucking do that?!"

Stella shook her head. "I don't know Riley."

He placed his hands on the table and shook his head in denial. He looked at her and swallowed, trying to gain control. "How do you know this?"

"It was in the letter that Jasmine left for me. She left one for me and another for Adam, after the adoption was final.

"I was working at the school in the daycare. We have to work with the babies on a rotational basis. A lady would bring in a little boy and I thought that he was the prettiest baby I'd ever seen. She was older so I assumed that she was his grandmother. Later I found out that she was his foster mother.

"Adam was just eighteen months at the time. I started to become attached to him. I'd go in to the daycare even when I wasn't supposed to be working with the babies. He gravitated to me as well. Everybody started calling him my little boy." Stella smiled.

"I started thinking about maybe fostering children." In actuality it was Adam that she wanted. But even still she had begun to feel an empty space in her life that could be filled by a child. And fostering seemed the most likely way for someone who had no interest in being married or having a mate bring a child into her life.

"So I asked Adam's foster mother about the process of becoming a foster parent and that's when she told me that Adam was foster to adopt. But she wasn't interested in adopting children, only fostering them. There are a lot of kids in the foster system like Adam. She'd had him since he was three days old and no white families had adopted him once they knew he was multi-racial with a father that was listed as 'unknown'."

Riley's face grew tight. But Stella continued.

"But I wanted him. My friends and family thought I was insane. You just don't know how I lived my life before Adam.

"I was on a hustle to becoming a millionaire before the age of thirty. That was my goal. All I did was work and study and invest. But suddenly I was excited about a little baby with big grey eyes and the happiest smile that I'd ever seen." Her eyes softened and she smiled at the memory.

"Adam's foster mother actually encouraged me to become a foster to adopt mother for Adam.

And I did. I had him for nearly a year when the adoption became final. It was the best decision that I ever made. And then the letters arrived from Jasmine. A lot of birth mothers do that, but they typically leave them in the child's file for when he turns eighteen. The letters came to my house." Stella paused. "It's a long letter and I'll let you read it if you like. It's your right to read it."

Riley nodded once. "What did the letter say?"

"She wanted to explain that she didn't put Adam up for adoption because he was multi-racial. But she was young, focused on her career and that being a mother was not part of her plans. She said that she hadn't been irresponsible, either, and that she had always used protection during sex but that she was just one of those unlucky women that got pregnant even on the pill.

"She went on to say that her baby's father was a man that she had been dating for a few years, but he...had just dumped her and left her without any explanation."

Riley blinked. He straightened slowly and ran his hands across the stubble on his head.

"She did say that she wouldn't have wanted to keep the baby even if he hadn't done it. Being a mother would have destroyed her goals. And she didn't want to saddle her child's father with the responsibility. So she left him as unknown. And she said that she would have kept it like that but she thought that Adam might want to know. And it was the only reason that she told me your name."

She watched Riley as he once again began to pace. She could see the pain that this information was bringing him and the guilt tore at her. It wasn't her fault, it had been Jasmine's decision to keep this from him but how long had she known before telling him? Two years...

He cleared his throat and Stella realized that he was swallowing back his tears. "Jasmine wanted to be a lawyer." He kept pacing, not looking at her but she saw him scrub his hands over his face. "She was the smartest person that I knew. I had never known anyone so smart, let alone dated someone."

Dating Jasmine had been like winning a prize. He was at Eastern on a full ride. He was a star. The papers wrote about him, recruiters stalked him. He had his pick of any woman but Jasmine had looked at him and she had chosen him—and not the other way around; beautiful smart Jasmine wanted him, Riley Pranger from Cobb Hill in Estill County Kentucky.

It didn't matter to him one bit that she was black. But he had liked her brown skin. He liked the differences between them—even when he felt guilty for noticing those differences. And no, he didn't tell anyone from his family. He didn't intertwine those two worlds. And it wasn't out of a sense of shame that he was with a black woman but shame of his background. She had money and a proud lineage. Her father was a city councilman and her mother was a practicing attorney. All of her siblings were college educated. Why should she have anything to do with a bunch of rednecks? In the time that they were together Jasmine educated him and showed him a part of the world that he'd never been exposed to while on Cobb Hill.

Once she had called him a redneck because of his country accent and it had stung so deep that he'd warned her never to call him that again, because calling him that was no different then him calling her a nigger.

She had been appalled that he had used such a word in conjunction with her. She'd stormed out and he knew then that he had deep feelings for her when he sought her out and apologized.

She had understood once he'd explained about being poor and ignorant. He'd even told her enough about his family so that she understood that she should never want to meet any of them. And they'd gone on towards a future where in his fantasies they would make a power couple. He would be a pro-football player, she an attorney, they'd live in mansions and drive expensive cars and travel all around the world.

It was the life that he'd planned with Jasmine at his side. But then he'd been injured and it changed everything. She was beautiful, smart and had a promising career and future. But he was now just a kid with no future and a shitload of debt.

He'd returned to Cobb Hill broken in body as well as spirit. And just like he had never intertwined his life at Eastern with that of Cobb Hill, he did the same once returning home. He never spoke to Jasmine again.

"Did you love her?" Stella asked when Riley finished the story. He hadn't meant to reveal so much but...why the hell not? What did he have in this moment but this tale to this woman that had just changed his life?

"I loved her. Or I thought I did." But how did you let someone you love down so badly? How was that love? Maybe he had been too young and inexperienced to understand the true meaning behind those four letters.

He thought about Adam. He had a son. That smart, wonderful, beautiful little boy was his son. He met Stella's eyes again.

"Does Adam know?"

"No. Not about you but he knows that he's adopted."

"Because he ran back to the cottage as if he knew you were about to tell me something-"

"He just wanted me to ask you if it's okay if he watches television with you at your house. He uh…misses the big screen. The television at the cottage only plays the local channels."

Riley sat down slowly. "My son…wants to watch television with me. This is so very surreal. I don't know if it's actually sunk in."

"I understand. Believe me. I don't know how I'm going to tell Adam or how he's going to react. It changes everything."

Riley nodded. "Right. And what is this going to mean for us? I'm his father now. I want to help support him. But I don't want to step on your toes. I want to see him, too. I want to be a part of his life." He remembered what Stella had said about Adam's father not being a part of his life but how she wanted to change that and suddenly all of the emotion that had been bottled up suddenly broke free.

He covered his eyes with his fist and sobbed. But it wasn't just from a sense of sadness. He was overjoyed and proud and afraid and he felt guilt and shame. But mostly he was just shocked.

He cleared his throat. Stella was now sitting next to him, rubbing his back and neck tenderly.

"Sorry," he apologized and chuckled. "I have a son." He gave her a crooked smile and she gave him one in return.

Chapter Nineteen

"I need to wash my face," Riley said while wiping his face with his palms. "But I want to see him. Is it okay? And I want to be there when you tell him. Please."

"Yes, you should be there." He went upstairs and washed his face. He looked in the mirror and pictured Adam's face. His son...

His heart beat in his chest and it felt as if he'd never felt a heartbeat before. Why did everything feel so new? He felt good. This is what it felt like to be a parent. His love for Adam had bloomed from nowhere into something that was now so big that it took up his entire perspective.

He dried his face and then hurried down the stairs and over to the cottage. Adam answered the door with a hopeful expression on his face.

"Hi Riley. Mom said it's okay if I come over and watch television with you some time. We can watch ESPN. Mom doesn't really like sports."

"Adam, will you let Riley in?" Stella called out in amusement. She was sitting on the love chair. The Bluetooth speaker was back to playing more R&B. He liked it and the way the cottage seemed so full of life now that Stella and…and his son were here.

He smiled at Adam. He was big for a five year old. He got that from his old man. "We can watch whatever you want to watch."

"Can we do it now?" Adam asked in excitement.

"Adam, remember what I told you-" Stella warned.

"It's fine. I have a few hours before work." And thank God there was a job to go to since he now had a little boy to support. He wanted to laugh out loud at the thought. Oh my God, he couldn't wait to tell Sully…

Oh shit.

The smile fell from his lips. Riley frowned. I have a black son. It was the first time that thought had crossed his mind. It fucking sickened him that it had only crossed his mind in conjunction with his racist cousin and family history.

His eyes settled on Adam again and his anxiety fell away. He looked at Stella and smiled. "Shall we go now?"

Stella nodded and stood.

When Riley's eyes opened he blinked and then checked the time. It was just after four. He yawned quietly into his fist and then looked around. Adam and Stella were fast asleep on the couch. Adam's head was thrown back and his mouth was open and soft snores issued from him. A proud smile spread across Riley's face.

Next to Adam was Stella. Once again her legs were folded beneath her and her head was propped on her arm, which rested on the couch's armrest. He got up from his seat in the armchair and tipped upstairs to the bathroom and to prepare for work. Before he got to the stairs he turned back and looked at Adam and Stella asleep on his sofa, in his house and for the first time in a very long time the house felt like a true home.

A home is made of people…

His eyes settled on Stella. She had done an amazing job of taking care of his son single-handedly, but was there someone taking care of her?

He went upstairs. Half and hour later when he had returned to the living room, Stella was awake and Adam's head was resting on her lap. He was still fast asleep.

"Hi sleepyhead." He greeted her. He sat down on the couch, placing Adam's feet on his lap.

"Sorry for falling asleep," she yawned. "It was a rough day."

Riley had to agree with that. "No worries. I napped also." He reached out and gently stroked Adam's short curls. "Jeez..."

"Still hard to believe?" Stella asked.

"Well it helps that he looks like me. How did I miss it?"

She chuckled. "Who would think that they had a son with a woman that they'd never met."

"True." He patted his son's legs and then examined his fingers. "He's got my hands too. Look at those nails. I guess he's got a habit of biting them too."

"I try to discourage it but I can't always catch it. He bites them down to where they sometimes start to bleed."

Riley's brow gathered and he had a flash of memory again. It was of Sully being punched repeatedly by his father. What kind of man would do that to his own son? But that's when the nail biting began for him. He felt a surge of protectiveness at the thought of anyone hurting his son or even Stella.

He saw the witch's finger sticking out of Adam's pocket. He had shown it to Riley while they watched television. They had ended up watching a kid's channel and Riley had been completely intrigued by it. He realized that kid's shows were also low-key geared to adults.

Adam had waved the witch's finger at him and had included him in the family's protective spell. Riley got up and dug through his desk until he found a length of string. Then he tied it securely around the finger and knotted the ends. Stella watched as he slipped it carefully around Adam's neck.

"There." He whispered. "Now you're protected."

Stella watched him. She'd made the right decision. The expression on his face was different than when she'd first met him. She couldn't explain it, but he seemed to have come to life.

"We better get going." She made to lift Adam but Riley gently picked him up.

"I got him." Adam sighed in his sleep and then rested his head against Riley's shoulder. Riley took a moment to press his cheek against Adam's head and then he carried him to the cottage. Once in the loft he placed him carefully on his bed and then slipped off his sneakers and lined them up against the wall.

Stella was still downstairs so Riley took a moment to scan the room that his son had claimed for the summer. There were video games, some clothes and shoes strewn about. A typical boy's room.

Riley went downstairs and Stella was pouring herself iced tea. "Do you want something to drink?" She asked.

"No. I better head out for work. When do you think we should tell him about me?"

"Do you work tomorrow?"

"Yea but in the evening. We can do it in the morning. Can we have breakfast together?"

"Yeah. Come over about eight?"

"I didn't mean for you to have to cook. I can make us some ham and eggs."

"That's right. You do cook."

He nodded. "I do fair to middlin'."

"Okay. Well we'll be at your house at eight."

He nodded once and then headed out the door. Before closing it he turned back to her. "Thank you for this Stella. Thank you for telling me. You didn't have to."

"It was the right thing to do."

His eyes locked onto hers. Stella didn't move or look away until he finally turned and left.

She pressed her back against the closed door. Her heart was beating a mile a minute. Stella. Stop.

She was attracted to him.

She rubbed her hands across her face tiredly. This wasn't about her. It was about Riley and Adam. She didn't need to try and create something between her and Riley just because he was Adam's father. She wasn't good with relationships. And the last thing that any of them needed was to create strain between themselves once they attempted a relationship only for it to fail.

Besides, he was white. And he'd already been in a relationship with one black woman that he had carelessly dumped. He was probably a good person—she had no doubt that he was. But his record with black women said that he was a lousy partner.

She thought about Evan. Maybe she had been too harsh. Maybe she would respond to one of his Facebook posts…maybe.

Chapter Twenty

"I thought you said that we shouldn't bother Riley too much." Adam stated as they walked to the main house.

"Well he invited us to breakfast. I guess that means he likes having us around, right?"

"Yep." He replied.

Stella chuckled. He'd gotten that particular expression from Riley. Adam walked into the house without knocking and headed for the kitchen. Riley poked his head around the corner and greeted them with a brief wave.

"Hey. Good morning," he greeted.

"Hi Riley. Thanks for making this necklace." Adam stated while gripping the witch's finger that was now hanging securely around his neck.

"Not a problem buddy."

Stella closed the front door and sniffed. "Mmm. It smells good in here."

"That's the ham and red-eye gravy." Riley disappeared back to the kitchen with Adam.

She watched him at the stove tending to the ham. "Are those homemade biscuits?" She asked in surprise.

"Yep." He turned to Adam. "Adam, why don't you grab something for everybody to drink? I'll have orange juice, please."

Adam opened the refrigerator and retrieved the orange juice. "Mom what do you want to drink?"

"Orange juice is fine."

"Can I have a Coca Cola?" He asked. "Riley has a whole bunch in here."

Stella scowled. "No. You can have orange juice or milk."

He knew she would say that so he didn't complain. Riley told him where the glasses were and he set the table.

"Stella, can you grab the biscuits and grits and put them on the table, please?" Riley asked as he began cracking eggs into another skillet which had a pat of butter sizzling in it.

She lifted the lid from the small pot of grits and eyed the perfect biscuits. She was tempted to steal one but Riley was giving her the side-eye. She just grinned at him and played innocent.

As they sat to eat, Stella admired the table and the food. "This looks wonderful."

Riley began scooping piping hot eggs onto his plate. "Let's see if it tastes as good."

It did.

As they ate Riley told them that he wanted to take them to the Fitchburg Furnace.

"Today?" Adam asked hopefully.

"Not today, but maybe Saturday. If that's okay with you mom."

"I think that sounds like a nice plan. I've wanted to see that place since I read about it online."

Adam buttered his third biscuit and than topped it with homemade jam. Riley exchanged looks with Stella, sending her a silent question. Stella cleared her throat and realized that she was suddenly nervous. Why would she be nervous? Adam liked Riley. Still this was big news for a little boy.

"Adam."

Adam looked up at his mom. "Yeah, mom?"

"I have something important to tell you."

Adam took a big bite of biscuit. "Okay."

"Don't talk with your mouth full," she said distractedly. "Adam. You know how I told you that I wanted to come up to Cobb Hill so that you could get a taste of country living?"

Adam nodded instead of answering.

"Well there is more to it than that." She and Riley exchanged looks and he encouraged her with a smile. "Remember the letter that your birth mother left for you?"

"Yes." Adam said slowly.

"Well in the letter she told us the name of your father. Your biological father."

Adam watched her.

"So I thought I'd come up here to meet him. Because the letter said that your biological father didn't know anything about your existence. I wanted to tell him about you in person."

Adam seemed to think about her words. He remained quiet so Stella continued.

"I met your birth father and I told him about you. He was very happy to find out that he had a son and he was happy to know that *you* were his son."

Adam's eyes flitted to Riley. He looked worried.

"Is...is it Riley?" he whispered hopefully to his mother. Riley swallowed back his chuckle.

Stella smiled and nodded. Adam looked at Riley and saw that he was smiling as well."

"Is this a trick?" Adam asked and then his eyes welled up with tears and he began to cry.

"Oh honey, no." Stella said as she reached out to comfort him.

Riley was immediately out of his chair and kneeling besides Adam. "Adam, it's no trick, son. I'm your dad." He lifted the boy and hugged him. Adam's arms went around his Dad's neck.

Riley stood. He was filled with so much emotion as he held his crying son in his arms. He hugged and kissed the boy, soothing him with gentle words. "Why are you crying?" He asked.

"Because..." Adam explained and then his tears began to ease back.

"Because why?" Riley asked, pulling back enough to look at him. Adam's face was streaked with tears and Riley reached up and brushed them away. "Because why?" he asked again.

"Because I wanted a daddy and I wanted it to be you."

Riley's face broke into a grin and his own eyes began to glisten. "Guess what?"

"What?" Adam asked.

"I cried when I found out that you were my son. I cried because I was so happy."

This time it was Adam's turn to smile. He hugged Riley tightly.

Stella discreetly wiped away the tears that were streaming down her cheeks. Riley looked over at her.

"Come on over here Mom. Group hug."

She laughed and joined them in the first ever Pranger/Burton group hug...the first of many.

Later, Riley followed them to the cottage where Adam wanted to show him some of his favorite video games. He sent Adam upstairs to get the game started and then he reached out and took Stella's hand. He placed in it a folded piece of paper.

She looked at him curiously. Because just the touch of his hand had sent tingles up and down her spine, but when she felt the slip of paper against her palm it had taken her back to reality.

She unfolded the paper and saw that it was a check for one thousand dollars.

"Riley," she said. "I don't want this back-" she tried to hand it back to him.

"I won't take money from you, Stella." He took her hand and gently folded her fingers around the check. "You've been taking care of my son all of this time. I won't accept your money for bringing him here to see me."

He turned without another word and jogged up the stairs to join his son in playing video games. The sight of his broad back as he jogged up the stairs momentarily took her breath away. He was gorgeous, sun bronzed, bearded and huge like a Viking.

She thought back to the feel of his hands on hers and felt a warm tingle travel across her body.

She frowned and shook away the ideas that had been swarming through her subconscious.

For the remainder of the week the three of them found every opportunity possible to spend time with each other as they could, going to Michaels for lunch, getting soft serve ice cream at the Twin and they even made a trip up to the Fitchburg furnace even before Saturday.

In the evening Riley went to work at the hardware store but spent most of his time there thinking about nothing but Adam and Stella. Luckily his job was easy, cashiering until the store closed and then completing inventory and stock.

His feelings for Stella were growing and although he knew that it was wrong to intertwine his feelings of love for Adam with his feelings for Stella, it simply couldn't be helped. Stella and Adam were a packaged deal for him. He didn't consider one in his life without the other.

He knew that he wanted to pursue something with her, although he didn't know exactly what. What could he be to her if he lived on a mountainside in Kentucky making barely twenty-five thousand dollars a year?

How ridiculous was he to think that he could be a part of her life? But sometimes when he looked into her eyes he saw that she watched him with more than just a polite indication that she was listening to his words.

He saw that her eyes lingered on him. And when that happened he could feel a spark that ran between them, connecting them. He absolutely knew that she felt it because he felt it for her.

It wasn't just that he desired her, because he did. He could barely stop thinking about the way her body moved and how it must look beneath her clothing. It was more than that. She was his family. That's what the connection said. And he knew without a doubt that she felt it too.

And the idea that their family connection could one day involve some other man, being her man and that man calling himself Adam's father was impossible for him to fathom. Just as he could not see himself wanting some other woman to be his woman and having her act as his son's mother.

Stella, Adam, Riley; that's how he saw his present and his future.

Riley was thinking these thoughts and trying to figure out how he could let Stella know how deeply his feelings had grown for her, when he heard the door of the hardware store open.

It was nearly nine, which was closing time. Hardly anyone came in this late, which is why Mr. Harper allowed him to work the store alone in the evenings—despite the fact that his supervisor still didn't think he was experienced enough.

"Yo' Riley? You in here, boy?" Sully called out.

"Sully? That you?" Riley had been taking stock of the paint supplies and he rounded the aisle and saw Sully, Mut Jackson and Doo Doo McMahon practically falling over each other. He gave them disapproving looks when he smelled the liquor that they'd been drinking.

But Sully's expression brightened when he saw his cousin. He gave Riley a hand slap and a hug.

"Hey cousin. I heard you landed yourself a job."

"Yep." Riley replied.

"See," Sully grinned. "You were all worried for nothing."

Doo Doo picked up a paintbrush, which had a protective covering over the bristles and was pretending to paint the air with it.

"Hey! Watch out with that. Those bristles get jacked up easy." Riley took the brush from him and replaced it in the appropriate bin.

Doo Doo mimicked him mockingly. Mut was picking up and replacing the candy in the snack bin.

Riley hurried over and took a candy bar out of his hand and replaced it. "Look guys, the store is about to close and they don't allow anyone in after closing..."

"Well *about* to close and closed ain't the same thing." Mut said and picked up the candy bar again. "Ring this up for me." He demanded.

Riley blew out an exasperated breath but rang up the candy bar and then accepted the dollar and some change from Mutt.

"You been around Cobb Hill a lot these last few days with them boarders of yours." Sully said.

Riley gave his cousin a long look. "I thought we been over this. When it comes to my boarders it's my business."

Mut was leaning against the counter, eating his candy bar. "You sweet on that black gal?" he asked.

Riley continued to watch Sully. Sully turned to Mut after another moment. "Leave him alone."

He looked at his Riley again. "I just wanted to congratulate you on the job is all. "

Riley's brow drew together. His eyes never left those of his cousin. "Congratulations are in order for many reasons. Just found out that I have a son."

Doo Doo roared in laughter. "Hell nah! You got caught up, Riley, my boy?"

"Who netted you?" Mut asked while joining in the laughter.

"Well congratulations," Sully grinned. "Who's the proud mama?"

"A woman I knew in college."

"College?" Sully frowned.

"Yep, I found out that my girl had a baby and put him up for adoption."

Sully's expression grew serious and the laughter stopped. "You never knew about your kid?" He asked.

"Not until just the other day." Riley replied. The other fella's went around commenting how fucked up that was.

"How'd you find out?" Sully asked.

"The lady who adopted my son came up and told me." Riley replied.

Sully's lips pursed together as he studied his cousin. He turned suddenly to his friends. "Let's go everybody." He said gruffly. "It's past closing.

Don't want Riley getting fired. After all, he got a little boy to start paying child support for."

The men left and Riley followed them to the door and locked it, flipping the Open sign to now read Closed.

Chapter Twenty-One

When Riley left work that night it was well after midnight. There were only two vehicles parked in the lot. One was his and the other belonged to Sully. He went to his cousin's truck and climbed into the passenger side.

Sully was drinking from a mason jar containing some clear fluid. Moonshine, no doubt.

"You taking a big chance drinking that right in the middle of the street."

"Cops ain't patrolling here." Sully replied.

He offered some to his cousin but Riley declined. He never liked the hard stuff and moonshine was about as rot gut as you could get—especially the moonshine made in these parts.

"That kid with the grey eyes is your boy?" Sully asked without looking at him.

"Yep. Adam is his name. And he's my son."

Sully adjusted his position in his seat as if he was suddenly uncomfortable. "You had a black girlfriend while you were in college?"

"I did."

Sully just shook his head in confusion. "Why?"

"What do you mean, why?"

"Riley! You were a star! You could have had any girl you wanted. Why choose a nigger-"

Riley held up an angry finger. "Watch your mouth! Jasmine is black. She ain't a nigger and neither is my son."

"Oh my God..." Sully chuckled mirthlessly. He turned to glare at Riley. "You fuck 'em if you want. But you don't claim them! What's wrong with white women?"

"Sully, stop acting like you never knew that I wasn't like you. You know I'm not into all that white supremacy bullshit!"

"Bullshit? Buddy that is the knowledge that our family has grown from. We are superior as a race."

"Fuck that!" Riley yelled. "Prangers ain't nothing but a bunch of thieving illiterates!"

Sully's face flashed fire. But when he spoke his words were even. "We down on our luck. Lot of people got it better. Lot of people have done better. Lot of people been given better opportunities. But even being, what you would call, poor and illiterate, I am still better than the highest nigger and the richest Jew. They are mongrels and mongrels might get a hand up—but it don't make them a man!"

Riley looked at his cousin and he felt sick. He literally felt sick to his stomach. He'd heard this same shit spewing from people's mouths from the time he was born--from his Daddy and from his Daddy's Daddy. They had all grown up listening to the rhetoric. But everything they described turned out to be lies when he could clearly see that the only bad people he saw were his own kin. But Sully...he believed the rhetoric. He bought it hook line and sinker.

Sully took another drink of his moonshine but he was clear headed and far from drunk. He looked at his cousin with pity.

"You young. A millennial they call you. Those titles catch you into the same liberal trap that so many young whites fall into. They listen to jungle music, and believe in a monkey president and they think it's all right to lay with lesser beings. Niggers and Jews and Spics are a trap because they look almost like *us*. That's why they needed to be kept away from decent men and women like you and the rest of the whites—so y'all don't fall up and get trapped by the liberal nonsense!

"If the minorities stayed on their own side of the tracks then everything would be fine and I wouldn't have any problems with them. But them uppity ones feel like they should challenge the whites, the president, the police, this country with their 'Black Lives Matters' and their kneeling during the anthem! It's bullshit! Quiet as it's kept, the president's got an agenda. He then told us all when he said Make America great again. Before him the United States was heading down the shitter. But President Donald J. Trump knew what needed to be done to make America Great again. They can make fun of him all they want— just like they look down on me and mine, but in the end they gonna fear me. They gonna fear us!" Sully pounded his chest.

Riley watched is cousin. He was beyond saving. There was nothing that he could say or do that could change the deep hatred that Sully and people like him felt. He shook his head and opened his door.

"You tell anybody about that son of yours and a shit storm is going to get brewing."

Riley swung back around with fire in his eyes. "You threatening me?"

"I'm warning you, cousin. I'm warning you. I can't protect you from this."

Riley was trembling with rage when he pointed his finger at Sully. "If you or any of your asshole, shit-for-brains, idiot friends come anywhere near me or my kid I'll shoot first and ask questions later! YOU GOT THAT?!"

"I ain't here to do you no harm!" Sully shouted. "I could have took you out all ready if I wanted that. I'm here to warn you, is all."

Riley climbed out the truck and slammed the door shut. He began stalking back to his own truck. He stopped and pointed at Sully. "I'm telling everybody about my son—everyone that I meet! I'm not ashamed of him. And if anyone comes for me, I will take that bitch out!"

By the time Riley arrived home, he was so angry that he was trembling. Twice he'd nearly ran off the side of the road. Before heading for his house he went to the cottage and checked that the front door was locked. It wasn't.

Goddamnit! He slipped inside. The house was quiet and there was only one light on in the upstairs loft that Adam must have been using as a nightlight. Riley locked the door and then checked the back door, which was also unlocked. Once he got everything locked up he kicked off his boots and settled himself down on the sofa.

It was much too short for him to stretch out on, so he propped up the pillows along the armrest and then allowed his feet to hang off the end. He covered his eyes with his arms and tried to relax.

He doubted that he would be able to sleep. When he did he kept seeing images of horrible things, his son wearing a hoodie and being shot while coming home from the grocery store. Stella being pulled over by a 'good ol' boy' and being carted off to jail only to be found hung in her cell. So many images that had one time been anonymous were now pasted on the faces of two people that he knew and loved and nothing could now wipe those images away.

"Dad?" Riley's eyes popped open. He looked around momentarily unsure of his whereabouts. But then he met the eyes of his son and he relaxed.

"Good morning." Riley sat up and stretched.

"What are you doing here?" Adam asked.

Riley scratched his head. "Thought I'd take you guys out to breakfast. There's a place called

The Last Stop diner that serves some mighty fine pancakes."

"Mom's still asleep."

"We'll wait for her to wake up." Riley said. "We can play some video games until then."

They were up in the loft when Stella came out of her bedroom yawning and scratching her armpits. She wondered what Riley was doing. He was probably up already. He got up each day at the crack of dawn.

"Adam?" She called from the foot of the stairs. "Call your dad and see what he wants to do today."

"Take you guys out for breakfast." Riley replied while peeking over the loft's bannister.

Stella jumped and hollered in surprise. She ran her hands through her messy hair.

"Sorry," Riley grinned. "Your front door was unlocked. If you don't want unwanted visitors you better start locking it."

"Uh...I'll keep that in mind." She headed for the bathroom to freshen up. An hour later they were walking into the diner.

Riley had been trying to decide how much he wanted to tell Stella about his conversation with Sully and he finally decided that he didn't want to tell her anything about it. He didn't even want her to consider that side of his life. He intended to keep them both safely away from the redneck side of Cobb Hill.

Which is why he had chosen to take them to breakfast at the little diner in Ravenna.

Trulane Henry greeted the newcomers. She recognized Riley Pranger and her mental safeguards snapped into place. It was something she did anytime she recognized a Pranger, remembering the first few weeks of her employment and the way Sully and his friends had come in calling her out of her name. When Clay found out about it he had gone off, breaking one of the offender's nose. Tiffany, the manager of the restaurant had banned the lot of them.

Riley hadn't been among them and he was a quiet one. He ate his meal, left a decent tip and then went on about his business. Still, he was a Pranger.

She was surprised to see that a tall black woman and a little boy accompanied him. She was pretty and the boy was clearly multiracial.

"Hi True," Riley said as he led them to the counter to sit.

True was surprised that he'd used her name. It was a first. "Hi Riley." She passed out menus. "Anyone want to start out with coffee?"

"None for me." Riley stated and Stella shook her head.

"True," Riley said before she could turn away to give them time to look at the menu. "I wanted to introduce you to my son, Adam." He said proudly.

Her brow rose before she quickly masked her surprise. "What a handsome young man you are." True stated. She held out her hand to shake and Adam shook her hand with a broad smile. Adam liked it when Riley called him son.

Riley turned to the tall woman. "This is Adam's mom, Stella."

The two women shook hands. "Nice to meet you Stella."

"Same here, True. That's a pretty name."

"Thank you. It's short for Trulane."

True returned to the kitchen with her eyes wide as saucers. "Jeb," she said breathlessly.

Jeb paused in tending to his skillet of scrambled eggs. He took one look at her face and then glared through the past-through. He saw Riley Pranger.

"What happened? That asshole up to no-good?"

Jeb was old enough to be her grandfather but he sure wouldn't allow anyone to harass her. He'd once taken a rolling pin to a man's head. In that way he had symbolically become her grandpa--her Caucasian grandpa.

"No. You won't believe this. That little boy is Riley Pranger's son!" She whispered.

Jeb frowned. "What you say, girl?"

"He just told me. He said 'this is my son Adam and his mother Stella'. I shit you not!"

"There's a black Pranger in the world?" Jeb asked incredulously.

"Seems so."

"Lloyd and the rest of them probably jumped up out of their graves up on that hill," he chuckled.

True just shook her head and returned to the front to take their orders.

Word of the first 'known' black Pranger in Estill County spread rapidly. It wasn't that True was able to spread the information so fast on her own, it was because Riley did. He took Stella and Adam around town, each time introducing them to the people they met.

They went to The Wal-Mart and got a bathing suit for Adam (Stella could not be convinced to purchase one or to be included in the barbaric practice of swimming in a creek). By the time they left the store he'd introduced them to over twelve people. Those twelve people told at least ten and. And on and on it went. And that is how everyone in Estill County knew about the first black Pranger before even the end of the day.

Chapter Twenty-Two

Shaun's back ached. She was tired but she couldn't complain. Bodie was equally overworked and near exhausted. He'd gotten his pal JD to help him out at the garage but JD just didn't know as much about cars as Riley and Pete had. In addition, he wasn't one for working hard, especially in the dead of summer when the heat topped one hundred degrees.

She'd been with the girls non-stop and she needed a break. Even half an hour to take a bath without them knocking on the door to find out what she was doing would have been a blessing. They ran amuck and she had to constantly keep after them. If they went out of sight for even a minute the baby would have a penny stuck up her nose a knife in hand preparing to stick into an obscure outlet that didn't have a cover.

She'd just put them down for a nap and was planning to take one herself when someone knocked on the door. They also rang the bell as if you had to do both.

She buried her fist into the small of her back and stretched waiting for the satisfying crack and pop. Oh, yes...She sighed in contentment and answered the door.

It was Angie, Theresa's mama, and she was holding little Jace's hand. Jace looked like he had been crying for a long time and then had gotten completely tuckered out from it. His little tanned face was swollen and still wet with tears and his breath was hitching in his chest as he sucked on a pacifier and watched her with big tired eyes.

He was a little over a year old and had always been a happy baby. So it was surprising to see him in such a state. Shaun frowned at Angie. She never had liked that woman. She'd heard her and her husband say some pretty nasty things about Theresa for 'ending up with that Mexican'. It sure wasn't going to be easy for Theresa living with her parents when Pete got deported.

"Hi Angie. What brings you here?" That's when Shaun noticed that there was a duffle bag also at Angie's feet.

"Theresa up and ran off with her cousin. She left this one here and I ain't got no time to be raising nobody's child. So I'm bringing him to you." The woman jerked the hand holding onto little Jace's toward Shaun and Jace cried out in pain, his pacifier falling from his mouth as he began to wail.

"Jesus." True said and then reached down and swooped the baby up into her arms. He was wet, his diaper was soaked through and he smelled like urine and sweat.

Jace immediately let out a deep sigh and stopped wailing. His eyes were hooded and it was obvious that he was exhausted. Shaun held him even closer.

"Where's Theresa?" She asked in confusion.

"Ain't you listening? She been messing around with one of her own cousins. I knew she weren't no good once she laid up with that Mexican. Now she been running around with my sister's boy and he ain't but seventeen. They ran off together and she left the boy with me. She ain't no goddamn good." Angie sighed and looked at Jace. "I'm too old for this." Although she was barely forty, she did look ten years older than that. "So you might as well take him to his father. They can go off to Mexico together. Theresa don't want neither of them no more."

"Oh Jesus," Shaun said while hugging Jace.

Angie turned away but then stopped. "Oh. And Theresa and my nephew were the ones that called the immigration people on Pete so they could get him out of the way. He better off without her." She finally left. Shaun stood there in total disbelief long after Angie and her husband, who was waiting in the car, drove off.

How had she been such a bad judge of character? She had liked Theresa. She had given her clothes and helped her with Jace.

The baby had fallen into an exhausted sleep against her chest. She carried him upstairs and placed him on her and Bodie's bed while she got a disposable diaper and items to give Jace a bath. When she removed his diaper she saw that his unchanged diaper had caused angry red welts to appear on his bottom.

"Jesus…" Shaun said again. This time she took time to study him closely and saw that his arm was swollen and she remembered the way he had cried out when Angie had jerked it. She covered him with a blanket and hurried to the phone. She didn't realize that she was crying until Bodie said hello and the words came out all garbled.

"Shaun?" Bodie asked. "Is that you, baby? What's wrong?!"

"Come home NOW! I think those bastards broke Jace's arm!"

He didn't say another word. The phone was dropped and he was in his truck within seconds.

The emergency room nurse stated that Jace didn't have a broken arm but a case of nursemaid's elbow. The slipped ligament was easily put back into place when the nurse slightly bent his arm at the elbow.

Bodie was pacing in anger. The girls were with his mother and he'd sent JD home and told him to close and lock up the garage. He was going to keep it closed for the time being. Shaun had told him the story about what Theresa had done. She'd also run off with the money that they'd given her to take care of herself and Jace. The little conniving bitch, he thought bitterly.

Worse is that the hospital was forced to call the police and a social worker had shown up threatening to take Jace into foster care.

"We're the only family he has. Isn't there some way for me and my husband to take care of him?" Shaun pleaded.

The social worker wasn't much older than Shaun. She was a white woman with round rosy cheeks, warm brown eyes and an easy smile that had disappeared when she learned the extent of the story.

"So the mother took off to pursue an incestuous relationship with a minor. The father is in the process of being deported. And the only other relatives left the child dirty, hungry and injured on your doorstep. Do I have everything correct?" She asked while scribbling in a notebook, her voice clipped and angry. "Unbelievable." She muttered to herself.

"Well," Shaun added as she rocked a sleeping Jace in her arms. He was now clean and fed and no longer seemed to be in discomfort. "The baby's mother was the one who called the immigration officials on Pete. And the grandmother doesn't care if they both are deported to Mexico. It's not possible is it? Jace was born here. What happens to him when his father is deported?"

Bodie was sitting next to Shaun now, his arm around her shoulders.

Miss Bruner, the caseworker shook her head. "This is out of my realm. What we can do is issue you temporary custody under Kinship Care. It's where close friends or family take emergency custody of the child."

Shaun nodded in relief. "So Jace can come home with us?"

"Yes. But this is temporary. I'll contact the magistrate and have him contact the immigration judge. We need to put an immediate halt to the deportation proceedings until Mr. Rodriguez can issue you temporary guardianship."

"Thank you, Miss Bruner." Bodie said. "Pete's going to be totally devastated when he learns about all of this."

Miss Bruner looked at the sleeping baby in Shaun's arms. "It's tragic how cruel people can be to each other."

Shaun placed her head on her husband's shoulders and closed her eyes tiredly.

Chapter Twenty-Three

The next few days were a dream come true for Riley. He spent his days with Stella and Adam and the evenings working at the hardware store — where there was air conditioning! Yeah the money sucked and his supervisor had another year of high school but life was now made up of more than just routines.

He was learning more and more about his son and Stella gave him the space to do it. They played video games but that didn't entail taking advantage of the fresh air. So he thought of more outdoor activities. He had even brought home a brand new football and they tossed it around for a while as Riley gave him pointers about playing the game.

Adam was even open to learning how to swim, although Stella still refused to do more than put her feet into the lake. One terrible day, Adam splashed his mother drenching the front of her shirt. She didn't realize how transparent the material was and for the next half an hour Riley had to stay waist deep in the water to hide his boner.

While Riley appreciated Stella giving him time alone with Adam, he also wanted to spend time with her. So he always found excursions that would include them both, such as putt putt golf, hiking, and on Saturday there was a festival down in Irvine that he wanted to attend.

They did talk some about the future, even child support--a topic that she shied away from. But he insisted that he'd send her a monthly check and it was up to her to decide what she would do with it.

Stella was very open about visitation and even invited him to visit them in Cincinnati over the Christmas holiday. He was quick to accept. He wanted to get a feel for how they lived. He told her that he hoped they'd spend at least part of each summer with him — at the cottage, that is. She seemed agreeable with that.

Riley decided that it was time for him to tell her how he felt. Stella trusted him with her most treasured possession, their son, so that most mean something. And he had caught her looking when she didn't think he had noticed. Also there was that strange, yet enticing pull that had begun to feel erotic. More and more it was becoming harder and harder not to lean forward and capture her lips when they talked quietly together.

He wanted to touch her skin and run his fingertips down her back. But each time he thought he might be bold enough to do it she would break the connection by looking away.

Saturday afternoon as he tossed the football with Adam in the front yard he was thinking about the best way to approach Stella when a truck pulled into the drive-way.

He scowled in recognition. It was Bodie Matthew's truck. Adam stopped playing and peered at the big man that exited the vehicle. He would have preferred if Adam had kept playing so that he could ignore the man but he supposed that wouldn't be very polite.

"Adam, go inside for a while so I can take care of some business. I'll be in shortly."

"Okay, Dad." Riley felt himself smiling at that word. It was his new favorite thing in the world, hearing his son call him Dad.

Bodie walked up to him, eyeing Adam curiously. "I heard you had a son. Guess that rumor is true."

"Yes. That's my son. Adam. He's five years old."

"Fine looking boy. Big for a five year old. Guess he takes after his daddy."

"I reckon he does."

Bodie didn't speak for another moment. The son of a bitch wasn't going to make this easy for him.

"I guess you heard about Theresa running off with another man."

Riley stared at him. "Heard about it."

"You probably heard that it was her that called immigration on Pete."

"I heard talk."

"Well it's true. And I wanted to come up here and tell you that I'm sorry for accusing you of having anything to do with it just because your last names Pranger. I shouldn't have fired you Riley and I'm man enough to admit that. If you want your job back, it's all yours. And I hope you'll accept my apology." Bodie held out his hand for Riley to shake.

Riley worked his tongue around his gum and then gathered up enough spit to let go a wad a Bodie's feet.

"I'm sorry too," Riley said. "For what I said about your family. It's not their fault that they got a fool for a man and a daddy. You can take your job and shove it up your racist ass."

Riley turned and stalked back to the cottage, slamming the door after him. Stella had been on her laptop and she jumped to her feet and hurried to Riley.

"What's wrong? What happened?" She heard Bodie's truck start and burn rubber as it pulled out of the drive-way and back down the hill.

"That was just some old news." Riley said. He gave her a smile. "It's done with." He clapped his hands together suddenly. "Let's go to the fair. There're some foot long hotdogs calling my name!"

Stella had never been a huge fan of fairs. She never saw the appeal in overpriced drinks, dangerous rides and questionable food. But she had apparently never gone with the right people. Riley and Adam had so much fun that she had no choice but to have fun as well.

Over the last few days Stella had begun to see things in a new light. She'd been all over Estill County and seen all kinds of people and what she had learned is that everyone was different either in the manner that they spoke or the way that they reacted to new things, but it didn't mean that they couldn't accept each others differences…that she shouldn't accept others differences.

She opened her eyes to the man that Riley was, and that allowed her to open her heart. If nothing else, she was willing to give herself a chance to see him with more than a jaded history of what white America had always represented to her.

Stella loosened up and allowed herself to experience things that she normally turned up her nose at. They ate foot long hotdogs and greasy funnel cakes and played expensive fair games in order to win cheap trinkets. And they also rode on the rides.

Adam was tall enough to drive his own bumper car and he got a great deal of pleasure in hemming her up against the rails. Riley and Adam even talked her into getting on the Ferris Wheel even though she explained to them that the people who put up the rides at a festival were typically just some homeless guy that the carnival paid a few bucks to and those guys didn't care if they lost a screw or didn't screw in a bolt.

Riley explained that this fair had come to town every year since he was a kid and he had never heard of one injury related to the rides— only some shooting and fistfights once it grew dark and the drinking occurred in higher numbers.

"Relax." He said to her as they rode the Ferris wheel. He placed an arm around her shoulder and goose bumps ran up and down her body. She didn't tell them that she was afraid of heights but having Riley's arms around her made her feel instantly safe. After a few moments she relaxed.

Riley looked over at Stella and Adam. He loved them. His arm tightened slightly around her and Stella finally leaned into his body. When they got off the ride Riley gripped her hand in his.

She looked at him quickly and he winked at her. After a moment she tightened her grip on his.

Tonight I will tell her. I will say; I have fallen in love with you Miss Stella Burton...

"You need to get up on out of here, boy! Don't nobody want to see that shit!" Riley felt something shove him from behind hard enough to cause him to nearly lose his footing.

He turned and saw his cousin Brady with three of the fellas that he ran moonshine with.

"What in the hell are you doing?!" Riley shouted. He shoved his cousin back. Brady was older and heavier but Riley was taller and broad with muscles. And in addition to that, he was now very angry.

Brady recovered quickly from the hard shove and he glared at his younger cousin. "You need your ass whupped for how you're carrying on with them mongrels!"

Riley punched him in the face. Two of his friends came for Riley but before anyone could lay a hand on him both men were stopped short, one by Bodie Mathews and the other by Lt. Christopher Jameson.

The Jameson's and the Matthews had caught sight of Riley and his little family and were about to make their way over to them. Bodie was reluctant having been recently called a racist by Riley. But the more he thought about it the more he realized that he had acted like a racist and Riley had every right to hold a grudge. He needed to make amends and he intended to do just that.

But Brady Pranger and his friends appeared and began his customary crap. Without a word Bodie and Christopher hurried to Riley's aid.

Riley had tackled Brady and they were both rolling on the ground. Stella pulled her son behind her.

"Stay back, baby." He was still more shocked than afraid but then he felt Brianna's hand slip into his. He gave her a surprised look and then squeezed her hand.

Stella's eyes were narrowed as she watched the fight. She wanted Riley to hurt the man. No...she wanted to hurt him. And then without a second thought she ran forward and aimed a kick at the big fat man that had called her and her child a mongrel. The well-aimed kick landed right on his temple stunning him.

"Stella, get back!" Riley growled as he flipped the man onto his back and held him down with his knee. He then punched him and continued to do so until Bodie and Christopher dragged him off the unconscious man.

Stella had dodged out of the way, but then she ran up and kicked the man again. "Nobody calls my kid a mongrel!" she screamed. Riley shook Christopher and Bodie loose and ran over to Stella, barely noticing the spike of pain in his knee. He grabbed her and held her.

"It's alright, hon," he said in a low voice that was still deep with unbridled anger. His eyes were on her completely. "No one gets away with that. No one." She was shaking so hard that her body quaked. She wanted to kill that asshole. Never was she going to lie down. She was going to fight all the way. She vowed it to herself and she vowed to all that could hear her.

"I'm never going to let someone get away with hurting us!" She growled. Riley's arms encased her, anchoring her to him. He kept staring into her eyes, speaking his agreement and soon her breath came out in even gusts.

"Damn." Bodie said in admiration. He liked Riley's woman.

Ashleigh and Shaun went to Stella, calming her while Christopher along with security carried away 'the trash'.

Chapter Twenty-Four

Stella was still shaking even though it was half an hour later. They were sitting in the family area around one of the picnic tables. Bodie was next to his wife while Ashleigh was holding Christopher Jr. as Christopher played in the clearing with all of their children, acting as both sentry and tackle dummy.

Even little Jace was toddling along after them, giggling and falling more than anything else. Bodie's girls were fierce and wild as they all played a game of tag, but Adam was careful and gentle with the smaller ones, especially when it came to Brianna. He was younger than her but he was bigger and he refused to tackle the girls, only allowing himself to be tossed to the ground by those wild ones (his nick name for Bodie's girls). Christopher liked Adam a great deal.

But at the picnic table things were not as easygoing. Stella had wanted to leave but Riley had taken one look at the expression of fear on his son's face and had asked to stay. He refused to allow Brady to turn this day into a bad memory for his son. He refused it. And reluctantly Stella had agreed. He was right, but she was done. She was done with Cobb Hill and Estill County and rednecks—and she was done with any fantasy that she might have had of a relationship with Riley.

Today had started off perfect. But she had forgotten the America that she lived in where racist felt they had every right to come up to someone different and spew hate talk. She and her son had to be warriors and she was not meant to be some passive black woman that shook her head at the reports of injustice. And she couldn't be with a white man who didn't know that there was a war brewing and that you had to take sides.

"I can't stand it here anymore," she finally said. She looked at Riley who was still holding her hand, as if she might fly off the handle if he didn't keep hold of her. He could feel the goose pimples on her skin and that her eyes were too bright. She was scared and she was angry. She slipped her hand from his and rubbed her goose pimpled flesh. Afterwards she kept her hands tightly clasped on her lap.

Shaun nodded her head at Stella. "I understand what you're feeling, Stella. Sully Pranger shot at me and Bodie while chasing us down Cobhill Rd!" She had only just met Stella but she understood the shock that she saw in the woman's eyes.

Stella looked at her in surprise. She barely knew how to form her next words. "Shot at you?"

"Bodie kinda laughed it off and I freaked out. I told him that I didn't want to be a part of this redneck town and I called him all kinds of names and told him to drive me to the bus station. I left and I had no plans of returning."

Bodie's face was growing red. "It was a little more involved than that. I wasn't trying to laugh it off. Up here in the mountains we are a special kind of crazy."

"Yeah," Shaun said dryly. "Where shooting at each other and driving off the side of a mountain is part of the fun." She turned to Stella. "The point is that there are some crazy dumbasses out there. But those people are gonna be everywhere. All across the world you hear about terrorism and hate."

"I'm tired of it! Every time blacks do something to bring focus on what's happening to *us*, we're called aggressive and biased!" Stella practically spat. "I'm a militant black woman if I talk about it! If I tell you that I know that black boys and black men are targets than I'm talking about things that make white people uncomfortable!" She looked at Bodie and Riley.

"Well I don't care if whites are uncomfortable. *I'm* uncomfortable!"

"But these men aren't the enemy." Shaun said.

Riley looked hurt. "Stella I want to understand. I know that living on this hill is like a blanket where I don't see all that you experience. But I know what's happening out in the world. I have a son that's African American. Yeah he's multiracial, but here in America he is black. I want to do everything that I can to protect him."

"Then be honest." Stella said while turning to him. "Stop trying to hide behind political correctness!"

"So political correctness is wrong?" Riley asked.

"Yeah when you can't talk honestly because whites are so afraid of offending black people if they say that…black people…" she searched her mind "…dance better than whites!"

"What?" Riley said after a long pause.

Ashleigh coughed back a laugh and then tried to clear her throat.

Bodie opened his mouth and Shaun lightly elbowed him. This was the conversation that Riley and Stella needed to have.

"What I'm saying is that whites are so afraid of offending us that you can't even get to your truth."

"If you know about my truth Stella, then tell me what it is. So I can stop guessing." Riley snapped. He wanted to learn but why should he be punished because of it? And that's what she was doing, punishing him just because Brady had done something fucked up.

"You can't fix America until whites recognize that slavery fucked it up for us all." Stella said.

"Oh shit…" Bodie whispered. Stella turned to him.

"Well you don't agree?" Stella asked.

He looked at his wife for guidance or for perhaps her okay to add to the conversation. His wife seemed to be waiting for his response as well.

"In truth…" he looked at Riley who also was waiting for him to continue. He swallowed. "In truth, I wish blacks would stop bringing up slavery. How is that even still relevant? Everybody that owned slaves is now dead. Look, I'm as far from being a racist as I can get." He reached out and lightly squeezed his wife's hand. "I'm part Cherokee, I'm married to a black woman and I have two black children and another on the way. But it ain't right for blacks to be asking for reparations when they weren't even slaves." He looked at Riley for backup, but Riley thought it would be wise for him to say nothing.

Before Stella could speak Shaun did. "You don't know that slavery impacts us today? Right here on this mountain there were families that owned slaves. Can you imagine what it takes to be able to own another human being?"

"Not even to just own them, but to be able to convince yourself that they aren't humans." Ashleigh added.

"Blacks owned slaves too." Bodie said, "Just like the Native Americans, but I hear that blacks were much rougher on their slaves."

Don't say it, Riley thought. Don't you say it Bodie...but he did.

"Besides, not all white slave owners treated their slaves bad."

Shit. Even he knew how stupid that statement was.

All three women instantly stiffened. "So stealing someone from their home and working them without pay, breeding them like animals and selling their children off to make a buck wasn't bad treatment?" Shaun spoke.

"Maybe some slave owners didn't rape and beat their slaves, but the act of taking away your freedom is cruelty." Stella added.

"Besides," Ashleigh added. "Slave owners had to convince themselves that blacks weren't human in order to justify their actions. And when you strip away a man's humanity you don't want them to talk back, to fight for their rights, to voice their opinion — to prove that you are wrong."

"I would like to think that if I lived during the times of slavery that I would never have been that kind of man." Bodie said softly.

Shaun kissed his cheek. "So many people died fighting to end slavery; black and white. But whites rarely listened to the blacks. It was the white voices that made an impact on other whites."

Stella nodded her head and looked at Riley again. "So the history of slavery taught generations of whites that they once were able to own people like me. And people like me question how the difference in the race of a man can equate to them being treated as less than a dog. You don't string up dogs. But whites strung up blacks."

Riley frowned but he looked at Stella. "Because a dog can't talk back."

She sighed and nodded her head. "That's right, Riley. We began to talk back."

There was quiet. "When I was a kid I asked my mother how slave owners could torture black people, how they could live with themselves," Stella said. "My mother told me that it was because white people were incapable of knowing right from wrong. They even had to make simple, stupid laws in order for the rest of them to understand how to behave."

"And that's not racist?" Riley asked.

"You white people are the ones that shoot each other up in schools, and snatch each others kids so you can eat them. That's white people that do that kind of shit." Stella stated angrily. "You don't see black people burying a bunch of people in their back yards!"

"But there's no such thing as black on black crime?" Riley said sarcastically. This time it was Bodie that subtly shook his head at Riley.

Shaun frowned. "Why is it black on black crime? Or reverse racism? Crime is crime. Racism is racism. If a crime is committed in your neighborhood and you live in a black neighborhood than it's called black on black crime. There is statistically more crime committed by whites against whites."

"Because there are statistically more whites in the world. But the percentage of crimes that take place in black neighborhoods by black people is proportionately more..." Stella gave him a hard look. "I hear," Riley finished slowly.

"You hear right." Stella said. "And that's more than likely because blacks have systematically been routed to the worst neighborhoods and given the least opportunities. When we ask for programs to help us out of that hole that we were shoved into, we are told that it isn't fair to the whites who weren't pushed down into those areas. That we're taking jobs from a white person who already owned those jobs and only shared them with their own kind!"

Riley stood up. "The hell with this! I'm not taking the blame for shit that I don't have anything to do with! I didn't make any of these rules, Stella! I live in the same America that you live in and I know that young black men get shot disproportionately by cops. But I also know that if there wasn't a generation of thugs running around talking about killing the police and sagging their pants and talking with disrespect than those cops might not be so quick to pull their triggers!"

Christopher paused from where he was in the clearing playing with the kids and he looked over to where the adults were gathered. "Hold on kids. Be right back. Don't run off anywhere. Bri, you and Adam are the oldest so you're in charge."

"Okay, Daddy," Brianna said.

"And for the record. I have all the respect in the world for Colin Kaepernick." Riley said. "He has every right in the world to voice his dissatisfaction about the state of race in America. He's a black man, I'm not. I have no say in his choice to fight the injustices that he sees happening against his race. But do you think that the whites in America that are against him are against him because they don't think he has a right to voice his opinion? That they don't think that he might not even have a reason to protest? He lost a lot of whites who believe that if you live here you are expected to pledge allegiance!"

"Pledging allegiance is just a bunch of political, white, rhetoric." Stella said while standing." The two were nearly nose to nose. Bodie opened his mouth but Stella placed a warning hand on his and he wisely closed his mouth.

"I pledge allegiance to my family!" She said. "I work hard every day so that I can provide my son a good life and not so that he can serve in some war and fight battles created by little dicks who don't want to fight for themselves!"

"No." Christopher spoke. "You pledge allegiance so that if someone comes onto your land and threatens to take what you have worked hard for, to regulate when and what you eat, where you live or to take away the rights that you and your son have, your pledge of allegiance is your promise that you will do everything in your power to prevent that.

"If you're talking about Colin Kaepernick, that is the reason that it has so many people up in arms," Christopher said. "It's not just a racial divide. I work in the military with plenty of non-whites who don't like it just like I work with whites that totally get it. Now if we're *not* talking about Kaepernick then the pledge of allegiance is something that you might willingly want to make because if you go into a third world country and you see a woman stoned for learning how to read, or you see a child forced to join an army that slaughters people over racial differences, and you don't want to be one of those people, you might be inclined to fight against it. I pledge allegiance daily because that's my job." He looked at each of them.

"Now back to Kaepernick. That's not his job. It's his choice. And that's why I fight so that we Americans can make our choices." He looked over his shoulder. "Now I gotta get back to the kids. Bodie your girls need to join The Marines. They are some kind of rough." Maddie had just tackled her older sister who was just about to pop her one.

Riley blew out a breath. "Let's sit down." He said to Stella. She nodded and sat down.

"Will we ever be able to come to an agreement when it comes to race relations?" Ashleigh asked mostly to herself.

Riley thought about Sully and how completely he believed in his ideas. "Not if we're afraid to understand our differences." He looked at Stella. She shook her head and looked away.

Chapter Twenty-Five

Stella and Adam had packed up and returned home a few days ago. Riley didn't blame her. She said that Cobb Hill was a place that she just wasn't ready to tackle.

He had considered not continuing to think of Estill County as his home. He was young. He could move to Cincinnati and be closer to his son. But it didn't appear that he would be getting any closer to Stella. He had put his foot in his mouth and out of desperation had told her how he felt about her.

She had cut him down.

Too much had happened too soon and he'd chosen the wrong time to reveal his feelings. It had come off sounding as if he just didn't want her to leave. He hadn't wanted her to leave, not like that. But how could he argue against her reasoning?

Bodie had asked him again to return to the garage and this time Riley didn't spit on him. He said he would as long as he allowed him two weeks for Mr. Harper to find a replacement for him at the hardware store.

One thing that hit home after everything that had happened this summer is that he had learned that he couldn't just sit quietly by and let the world go crazy around him. He had to set some things right—at least those things in his reach.

The Sunday after Stella and Adam left he went to LovingCare to visit his granny. As he walked to the lounge he thought about her black friend. But back when she lived at home she referred to blacks as niggers and expressed nothing but distaste for them. What was real? Because one side of her personality wasn't.

Granny was staring at her hands and his expression saddened. He knelt beside her and sighed. "Hi granny."

She looked up at him in confusion. "Riley?"

He smiled. "Yeah it's me." He took her hand and kissed her crooked knuckles. Jewel Pranger looked at him and smiled but still seemed unsure. "Where am I, Riley? This ain't my house, is it?"

"No granny. You live in a different home now. You live with some of your friends in an elder care facility."

"Okay…" she said after a few moments.

"Granny…" he took a deep breath. "I wanted to tell you something."

"Okay." She said, although he wasn't sure if she really understood him.

"I have a son."

"You do?" She asked. She smiled. "That's good, Riley. Is the mama a nice lady?"

Riley nodded. "She is. She's a strong woman. She has a lot of ways like you granny."

"We a family of strong people." Jewel said. Her eyes seemed to clear a bit.

"You think so?" He asked doubtfully.

"Oh yeah! You had to be strong back in those days. You didn't have no grocery stores where you could just pick up a chicken. You had to wring its neck and pluck its feather just to eat. Then you had to make it stretch between your family and your husbands ma and pa."

He listened. "Granny my son is African American."

"What?" She asked in confusion.

"My son is black."

"Oh..." she said distantly. "You better not tell your daddy. Wait," she frowned. "Are you Riley?"

He nodded. "Yes ma'am."

"Oh. Your son is black, you say? I'm not sure if I understand all of this."

"Granny you never liked blacks when I was coming up. But you have a black friend now."

She frowned at him. "You can't like blacks and survive in our family. You see how my daddy beat my mama? He beat us kids the same way. You did what my daddy said or you got beat down. If my daddy called a nigger a nigger than he was a nigger."

Riley looked at a black attendant that had overheard her. "Grandma, your daddy is long dead. And there is no one around that will force you to think like that. If you want to like blacks then you can. But whether you do or don't, please stop using that word. The people here don't like it."

Jewel frowned. "No. It's not the right word. It's a bad thing to say." She looked at him and smiled. "Riley? Is that you?" She reached out and patted his beard. "Such a handsome young man."

He smiled. "I'm not that handsome, granny."

"Hush you! You got the Pranger eyes."

He smiled. "So does my son."

"Oh yes, you have a son. But you can't tell your daddy that he's a black. Your Uncle Lloyd might hurt him. Your Uncle Lloyd is just like my daddy. He hurt the niggers."

"Granny that word...we don't use that anymore. It hurts people. It hurts the people that work here and they are here to help you." Jewel blinked and looked around at all the black faces.

"Oh my…" She covered her face with a shaky hand. "Sometimes I forget things. I forget where I am."

"I know granny." He held her hand. "Granny, I have to ask you something."

"Sure, Riley. Are you okay?"

"Yes. But…it's about Sully and the rest of them."

"Mmm," she pursed her lips into one of distaste.

"Why don't you like Sully?"

"I don't like Lloyd. God knows he's my son but he's evil. He's as evil as my own daddy was. His kids didn't fall far from the tree!" She met his eyes and they were clear. "I didn't want any of them around you, Riley. They are a bad lot. When Sully touched you that time, I knew he would infect you with his ways. All of them got something off about 'em. They lay up with any man and breed like rabbits."

Riley's face began to pale. He remembered Uncle Lloyd punching and punching and calling Sully a faggot. *No son of mine…*

He had been about six years old and all the boys had been wrestling. Sully always played with them and he liked him because he didn't act like he was too good to play with them. But when they were playing Sully had held him too close and wouldn't let him ago. He rubbed his dick against him and it was hard. Bobby hadn't known what was happening and had jumped playfully on Sully who had then released Riley.

He had just been confused. He hadn't meant to tell on Sully. He told his mama about what had happened and his mama had told daddy. Daddy must have told Uncle Lloyd because he came raging into the house where Sully and his brothers and sisters usually came to spend the day during summer months.

Uncle Lloyd had grabbed Sully and started beating him right there in the kitchen where they all were getting a drink of water.

You touch another little kid you little faggot...

And the beating had continued until he had finally collapsed to the floor, his face unrecognizable. Nobody did anything. His mama had turned away. His daddy had just looked disgusted. But Uncle Lloyd had looked like he was enjoying himself.

Afterwards he had wanted to tell Sully how sorry that he was. He was so sorry for telling on him. He didn't even know if Sully realized that he was the reason that he'd been beaten. After that Sully was only 'yes sir, no sir' when it came to his father. All the kids were and not just the kids, so was Uncle Lloyd's wife Aunt Eva. Once he heard daddy and uncle Lloyd on the porch drinking and uncle Lloyd had said that Aunt Eva was ugly as a dog but she let him do whatever he wanted in bed. Daddy had told him to be quiet because mama and aunt Eva were sitting right there. Aunt Eva said nothing, she just looked down in shame.

He realized that his eyes were wet. "Why didn't you stand up for Sully?" He asked.

"Sully?" His grandmother said dismissively. "Because his father had already ruined him."

Sully answered the door of his trailer in surprise. Riley was the last person that he expected to see visiting him.

"What are you doing here?" he asked and let a mouthful of chew go flying to the floor of the porch.

"I wanted to talk to you. Try to clear the air about some things."

Sully regarded him for a moment before pushing open the door to allow him inside the trailer.

"Get us a beer out of the fridge," Sully instructed while returning to his seat in his armchair. When Riley returned with the brews

Sully used the edge of the side table to pop the top. He took a swig and belched. He studied his cousin who took a seat on the couch, still holding his unopened bottle.

"What's on your mind? I heard about what Brady did, jumping you at the fair. I told you."

Riley scowled. "I don't give a shit about Brady."

"Well, that's good. He sure as hell don't like you no more."

"I ain't here to talk about none of that. My son is off the mountain so he can feel free to come at me with all he got. I came here to talk to you about something else."

"What?"

Riley licked his lips. He stared at Sully. "That time uncle Lloyd beat you. That was my fault."

Sully didn't speak, but his brow drew together.

"I told my mama about us wrestling and...how I felt your boner poking against me. I didn't...I wasn't tattling or anything. But she told daddy and-"

"Shit. What the fuck?" Sully scowled at Riley. "You think that was your fault?"

Riley swallowed. "I shouldn't have said anything."

Sully waved his words away. "My daddy beat my ass almost every day of my goddamn life. He called me nigger, faggot, bitch, pussy..." He shook his head. "Ain't your fault that he did anything that he did." Sully took a long drink. "His ass is in prison so look who the faggot is now." He chuckled mirthlessly, then he frowned at his cousin. "Why are you even thinking about any of that?"

"Sully," he scrubbed his hands across his face before he could meet his cousin's eyes again. "Nobody in our family did shit to help any of y'all...not even your own grandma and grandpa!"

Sully sighed. "That's because granny's pa did the same thing to her and to her husband and to their kids. By the time your daddy was born they had their own house. She protected your Daddy. My daddy thought he was a pussy. And he was."

Riley finally removed the cap from his bottle and he took a long drink of the cold beer.

"Why do you believe any thing that came out of the mouths of those people?" Riley finally asked. "They weren't smart. They were just a bunch of bullies that couldn't do anything but hurt their own women and children!"

"My daddy was a son of a bitch," Sully pointed a finger at his cousin, "but he was far from stupid. We survived when there wasn't shit to eat, and barely a shack to call a home. We survived it!"

"You give him credit for that? He fucking drank away all y'all money!"

"Hey!" Sully jumped to his feet. "Watch it, Riley! There's a lot that you don't know, that you don't understand!"

"Then tell me, cousin. Make me understand."

Sully frowned and sat down without another word. He shook his head. "You had it good, but you don't know it. You had food everyday. You had a place to sleep and you had a mama and daddy and a granny and grandpa. I had to work for everything I got, even if it was a morsel of food. But I was taught to be proud. When someone looked down at me I beat the shit out of 'em. Fear and respect ain't that far apart."

"Being a bully doesn't make you anything special, you know. So you run around trying to make other people's lives harder. Why? You know what it's like to work for everything you got-"

"You still talking about blacks? Boy it's a scientific fact that Aryans are the superior race-"

"You don't believe that." Riley said simply. "You just had to believe that so that you could have a reason not to kill yourself. You found a bunch of people that talked the same shit and you called those boys family."

"You think you're the same as a Jew?" Riley spat.

"You believed what your daddy beat into you, because it was the only way to survive. It was the only way to cope. That's why y'all never went too far away from your daddy or his abuse."

Sully glared at his cousin. "You think cuz you went to college that you're some type of psychologist?"

"You found a way to cope, to accept him, to even love him. He taught you ugliness-"

"I didn't love that bastard!" Riley was back on his feet. "I hated him! I hated what he did to me and my mama and my brothers and sisters. We are fucking survivors of a war that you or your family knew nothing about! I fought to survive!"

"But you learned from him! You learned to be like him!"

Sully glared at Riley.

"Are you proud to be like him?" Riley demanded.

"People respected him." Sully said. His eyes were red.

"No they didn't. They were scared of him-"

"Same thing." A tear dripped from Sully's eyes but he didn't notice. Riley did, though.

"He's in prison for killing people, raping and killing people—and not black people, *white* people. He wasn't superior. He was a monster."

Sully finally realized that there were tears in his eyes and he quickly wiped them away and took his seat. "I never said he wasn't a monster. And I don't want to be like him. I just want to be respected!"

"Respect is earned, cousin."

Sully stared at the television screen. "I'm better than mongrels. I'm better than niggers. I'm better than Jews." He said it as if it was a chant.

Riley finally stood. He headed for the door but when he was behind Sully's chair he placed a hand on the man's shoulder.

"I love you." He quickly left. He knew then that he would never talk to Sully again.

Chapter Twenty-Six

~December 2017~

Stella walked past Adam's closed door and heard him talking to his father. She lingered at the sound of Riley's deep country drawl. It still sounded as if his voice was gravel over honey. And the sound still caused her to feel that same strange electrical zing.

She continued on to her bedroom. Every night Adam Skyped with his dad before going to bed. It was the new age of co-parenting. But Riley and Adam could do a lot of things via Internet. For his sixth birthday, his father had sent him a cell phone of his very own. He called his dad anytime of day or night and for any little reason.

Stella didn't realize that Adam was doing that until one morning she heard him calling his daddy just to ask if he should wear Timberlands or sneakers to school that morning. When she told him that he shouldn't bother Riley while he was at work, Riley had overheard and instead of talking to her directly he had instructed Adam to tell his mother that he could call anytime day or night.

Things were a little tense between her and Riley. They hadn't left Cobb Hill on the best of terms. Riley had told her that he was developing feelings for her. And she had still been angry. She told him that she didn't want to be with a white man, no offense. None taken, he'd said snidely.

It was the truth. She didn't want to live her life with a white man that she had to explain why she felt and believed the way she did. Whenever something political happened she didn't want to have to wonder which side he was going to take.

She had returned home and had picked up things with Evan. That hadn't lasted long. She didn't like Evan and regardless of whether he had a good job and was handsome, he irked her for some reason.

But at least she was open to the idea of having a man in her life. She'd gone out on a few dates and the guys were mostly cool, but she didn't feel that...connection.

She knew the feeling that she was looking for because she had felt it before... But none of the guys sent an electrical zing through her nerve endings. They didn't make her heartbeat speed up. And they didn't cause her eyes to linger on the V of their back or the way their toned legs filled out worn jeans. None of them had slow country drawls that sounded like gravel and honey.

She and Riley did communicate—just not on Skype. Regular phone calls worked for them. Basically they were about Adam's classes and setting up a payment schedule for child support.

She knew that she'd pissed off Riley when she told him that he didn't have to send so much child support. She had the money to support Adam. He'd taken it all the wrong way and said that he had the money to take care of his child.

"I didn't mean to imply…"

"What? That I was a redneck that couldn't afford to keep my son living in the style that you've created for him? Don't worry. I didn't take it that way."

Riley was supposed to come to Cincinnati for Christmas—at least that had been the plan before things had taken a turn. Under the circumstances she didn't think she would feel comfortable with him there so she had contacted him and told him that she'd bring Adam and he could stay for a week.

"Are you sure?" Riley had asked, not wanting to get his hopes up too high.

It had pleased her to be able to do something like that for him. Besides, she might not trust the people on that mountain, however she did trust Riley to protect her son.

"Yeah. I'm sure."

"I'll come and get him-"

"No. You don't have to do that. We're going to be driving up from my parents place. We stay with them for a few days and celebrate on Christmas Eve with them. I can drop him off at your place on Christmas morning."

"Stella…I don't know what to say. It means a great deal to me. I'll drive him back home, though, okay?"

"Okay," she agreed.

"Thanks." He said and for the first time in a long time neither sounded defensive.

Riley rushed out to the shed for his axe. He needed to find a Christmas tree and then he needed to go through those old boxes for the Christmas decorations. He could have gone down to The Wal-Mart for matching decorations with perfectly painted surfaces and sparkles strategically placed. But he liked the homemade ornaments that they had made when he was a kid. He needed to see the old ornaments — to remember something good about his childhood.

Christmas was next Monday and he had plenty of time, but he still went out in the middle of the night with his flashlight and located the perfect tree, not too big but not too small. He took it to the shed to get it prepped and sat it in a bucket of water. Only once he was satisfied that it would be perfect did he return home and to bed. After work he'd run into town to finish shopping. He hadn't bought anything for Stella, but he would. He wanted her to have something to open on Christmas Day.

On Saturday he stopped at J&B's market and loaded his grocery cart with all kinds of things that he thought his son might like. Miss Lemon had looked at the contents of his cart critically.

"Adam coming into town?" She asked with a wink.

"How did you know?" He asked incredulously.

"Because you haven't purchased this much breakfast cereal since the summer when your son was in town." She wrung up his order and then threw in two large candy canes. "Stocking stuffer. You did get Christmas stockings, right?"

"Yes ma'am. I got stockings."

"Good. Bring him in if you get a chance. I want to see how big he's gotten."

"Yes. Thanks Miss Lemon. I will. Merry Christmas."

"Merry Christmas." He loaded his groceries to his truck and looked out at the clear sky. It would be nice if it snowed. He could have taken Adam sledding. But the temperature was almost balmy. Still, it was going to be a great Christmas, snow or not.

On Christmas Eve he Skyped with his son on his new cell phone. Adam showed all the Christmas things that he'd gotten from his mom and grandparents. "I got you something, too, Dad."

"You did?" Riley asked. Adam showed him a big box, which had been wrapped haphazardly with two kinds of wrapping paper.

"Did you wrap it?" Riley asked.

"Yeah but I ran out of paper. Mom helped me."

"Are you all packed?" Riley asked him.

"Yep. We gonna leave early in the morning. Mom said she wants to be at your house by 8 am so she can have time to get back home before the snow fall gets heavy. Did you hear, Dad? It's supposed to start snowing tonight in time for Christmas."

"That would be nice. If we get a few inches I'll take you out sledding."

"Cool!"

"Get some sleep. See you in the morning, son," Riley said. "I love you."

"I love you too. Goodnight, Dad."

He hung up feeling as if there wasn't one thing in the world that could match this feeling...and then he thought about Stella.

Chapter Twenty-Seven

On Christmas morning, millions of little children jumped out of bed and dashed to the Christmas tree to see what Santa had brought. But Riley jumped out of bed and dashed to the window. It was still dark out but he could see the light dusting of snow over the surfaces and the way it shimmered in the sky.

He smiled to himself. His son had gotten his white Christmas. He got cleaned up and ready for the day. Stella and Adam would probably be hungry so he made pancakes and ham and then kept them in the oven to stay warm. He made some hot chocolate and got out the marshmallows. He turned on the satellite radio, which was playing Perry Cuomo Christmas through his Bluetooth speaker. He fiddled with the dials until he found a channel playing R&B Christmas music. Mariah Carey was singing about all she wanted for Christmas.

He chuckled. All he wanted for Christmas was two simple things. One of them he was going to get...the other he would have to really work for.

He checked the time. It was nearly eight am. He threw another log onto the fire and then went upstairs to check that Adam's room was warm enough. He'd bought a space heater just in case it got too cold. It had been a pretty warm fall and this was the first real cold spell that they'd gotten. He wasn't surprised. Summer had been terrible with its heat index constantly reaching one hundred degrees. It might take a little time for the cool weather to settle in. January and February might give them hell.

He went back downstairs and appraised the Christmas tree. It was kind of old fashioned with its hand tied red ribbons that his mama had made from an old red dress. His brothers and sisters had made stars out of old cardboard and colored them in with crayons and dollar store paints. He appraised the Angel on top of the tree. It was the one store bought item. The Angel had a peaceful face and she held a candle—which no one ever dared to light for fear that the entire house would go up in flames.

He smiled to himself as he looked at the presents under the tree. With the smell and sounds and sights of Christmas Riley felt at peace in a home that had stopped feeling like a home, but which was just now beginning to regain that feeling.

He checked the time. It was nearly eight thirty. He went to the window and looked out. The sun was up and coated the yard in a beautiful kaleidoscope of colors. He opened the door and went out on the porch.

It was very quiet, as if the light snow had placed a muffled blanket across the world. He frowned and checked the time on his cell phone. It was eight thirty now.

He called Adam. The phone rang and then finally went to voicemail. "Call dad," he said simply. But now a worried crease had formed between his eyes. He called Stella. Her phone continued to ring as well.

That wasn't right. He knew that her phone was set so that she could use it while driving. She didn't have to dig for it through her bags or purse. He called again but hung up as soon as it once again offered him the opportunity to leave a message.

He dashed back into the house and quickly pulled on his boots. He then grabbed his coat from the hook by the door. He ran to his truck but the moment his feet landed on the cement he slid, nearly landing on his ass.

His face turned white. Ice.

Instead of continuing for his truck he dashed to the cottage and beat on the front door. Pete answered the door holding Jace on his hip. Jace was holding a plastic puzzle piece in his hand. Several other puzzle pieces where strewn across the parlor floor.

"Hey Merry Christmas-"

"Pete!" Riley said, "Call Bodie. Tell him that there's a wreck somewhere on Cobhill Rd, maybe Tipton. Tell him we need the wrecker."

Pete's eyes grew wide. "Your son?"

"I think they wrecked!" Riley was heading back to his truck. Pete wasted no time getting Bodie on the phone.

Riley started his truck. He pulled out carefully even though he wanted more then anything to go racing down Cobhill.

His phone rang and he dug it out of his pocket. Before he could speak to say hello he heard Bodie's voice.

"Where are you?!"

"I'm driving down Cobhill. I need you to start from Tipton and make your way up."

"Okay. Keep your head, Riley. It's slick as shit. I already fell on my ass once."

"I know. I gotta keep the line open."

"Okay. Call me."

"I will." He disconnected and placed the phone on the console. Please God...he begged.

He saw one other truck making it's way up the road and he blew at it like a maniac and jumped out his truck. The driver climbed out of his and met Riley half way. It was Mr. Pike. He had the best corn on the hill.

"Riley, what's wrong?" The older man asked.

"Mr. Pike, did you see an accident while coming up the hill?"

"No. No accident. But it's pretty slick."

"Okay, thanks!" He hurried back to his truck and nearly slid before he reached it. The ice was invisible beneath the fluffy snow. It didn't help that the snow was falling harder now.

"Riley!" Mr. Pike called. Riley turned to the older man who was making his way toward him. "Come to think of it, I did see something strange. I was following tire tracks in the snow but then there suddenly weren't any."

Both men knew what that meant. Someone had gone off the road. "Can you tell me where?"

"I can show you." The older man got back into his truck and drove a ways before he could turn around. Riley waited patiently and then allowed him to take the lead. Mr. Pete drove very slowly but he had to. There was no need for two vehicles to end up off the side of the road.

A few moments later Mr. Pete stopped. He got out and pointed and Riley could see the crushed snow and tire marks. Fresh snow had begun to cover it but it was clear that a car had gone off the embankment.

"Call Bodie Mathews!" Riley hollered as he ran to the embankment and then down into it.

It was a bad drop with fifteen feet of rocks and large stones leading to a grouping of trees and a small creek. There was a white SUV overturned on its hood. It had gone over the large rocks and was stopped from going over a second cliff by a group of trees.

"Stella! Adam!" Riley slid and fell and rolled down the hill until he reached the vehicle. The windshield was shattered. Stella was hanging suspended from her seatbelt, her body unmoving.

He tried to unlatch the seatbelt but it was jammed. He cradled her face. "Stella?" she was breathing but there was a gash on her forehead. Where was Adam?

"ADAM!" He screamed while looking around. He tried once again to unjam the seatbelt but it held tight. He looked at Stella and then scrambled away from the car. "ADAM?!" He called again. Adam had been thrown out, please God don't let the vehicle have crushed him…

He searched for his son's body. "ADAM!"

"Daddy…" He heard the soft cry.

"Adam!" He followed the sound to a grouping of trees fifteen feet away. Adam was walking to him, holding his arm cradled against his body. He was scratched but not bleeding and he was walking...on his own two feet!

Riley slipped and righted himself and then he grabbed his son in his arms and held him tightly.

"Oh my God," he cried. "Are you okay, son?"

"My wrist..." Adam said. Tears had left tracks down his ruddy cheeks. He wasn't wearing a jacket and one of his sneakers was gone. Riley placed him down and quickly took of his coat. He wrapped it around his son and lifted him in his arms.

"Riley! Is he okay?" It was Bodie. He was looking down at then from the road above. The wrecker's hazard lights were flashing behind him.

"Yeah he is, but Stella..." He hurried back to the truck. Stella was still hanging unconscious from her seat belt. A pool of blood from her head gash had formed on the console. It wasn't much but the sight of it caused Adam to cry and scream for his mommy.

Bodie was there in seconds. He whipped out a hunting knife and began cutting at the restraints. Riley held his son in his tight grip. When Stella began to fall from her upside down position Bodie caught her and carefully carried her out of the truck and away from the wreckage. He placed her down on top of the fresh snow. He could probably carry her up the embankment but it wouldn't be wise to do if she had broken her back or neck.

He loosened the turtleneck from her throat and then listened to her breathing to make sure that her airway wasn't obstructed. Her breathing was shallow but steady.

Adam was crying hysterically at the sight of his unconscious mother. Riley could only rock and sooth him with reassuring words. But he wasn't sure himself. Stella looked dead.

"Paramedics are on their way." Mr. Pete called from the street.

"Stay up there, Mr. Pete!" Bodie warned. He hurried to the upside down vehicle and located her coat in the backseat among a mess of gifts, luggage and overturned clothing.

Bodie covered her with the coat while flakes of snow fell into her hair and onto her lashes. As Riley stared down at her he thought she looked like an ice Princess, one that was in a never-ending sleep that even the kiss of a Prince wouldn't awaken her from.

Chapter Twenty-Eight

Stella's head was pounding. The doctor said that she might have a bad headache for a few days. She'd said it as if the feeling of a spike being shoved into your cranial wall was no big deal. Of course, the alternative was that she could be dead right now.

Adam was curled up in the bed against her, his thumb in his mouth. He hadn't sucked his thumb in ages. She looked at the cast on his left hand, which ran halfway up his arm and then she lightly kissed the scratches on his face. He was okay. Besides a fractured wrist he walked away from the accident with just some bruises and banged up from being thrown into the cushion of trees. He had indeed been flung from the vehicle.

She closed her eyes and fought back the image of the alternatives, the car rolling over on him, or God forbid, him landing twenty-feet to the ravine below. The guilt at being the person who might have killed them resurfaced. She saw her mistakes while driving the hill, the way that she had bear down on the gas to get past the patch of ice...

The door opened and Riley came in carrying a tray. It contained ham sandwiches and tomato soup.

"You ready to try to eat something?" he asked.

They were in the bedroom of his house where Riley had taken her after Dr. Wolf had given her a clean bill of health. She had a case of whiplash, bruises where the seatbelt had trapped her and of course a gash on her forehead where she'd received four stitches; a permanent reminder that one misstep could result in lasting damage.

Her car was totaled and that meant she and Adam were spending the next few days with Riley. She had told him that she was okay with staying in the cottage but he had explained that he had a renter.

She remembered the story about Riley being fired because he had supposedly said something to get his co-worker deported. Riley explained that it had all been cooked up by this fella's no-account wife who had reported him to immigration just so that she could run off with another man.

But the surprising turn of events is the letter writing campaign that the entire town of Cobb Hill had initiated. Nearly every resident had signed it, including many of the residents of

Irvine and Ravenna. After Pete's little boy was left with no guardian the immigration judge took in to account the number of signatures and instituted something called prosecutorial discretion—meaning that they just stopped the process of deporting Pete.

Riley didn't exactly understand it, but the way Pete explained it to him is that the courts were too busy searching for felons and violent criminals, and sending him back to Mexico was not worth their time. So, for the time being Pete was just being ignored by ICE. Not that he was completely safe. He didn't have a green card and once all the dangerous undocumented individuals were deported they would make their way back around to him. Of course he would probably be long buried by then.

"Your town did that for him?" Stella had asked as they made their way back up the dangerous hill.

"Yep. We aren't all bad."

She had ignored that comment. At the time she was too busy trying not to be sick at the sight of the winding road that had so recently nearly killed her.

Riley had driven it slower than he needed to, out of consideration for her. Adam was thankfully asleep.

"How did it happen?" He had asked when they reached the spot of the accident. There were emergency cones still set up on the edge of the embankment.

In all honesty she wasn't quite sure. They'd hit a patch of ice right before one of the many sharp turns. She hadn't been afraid until then. She had just wanted to get to the house as quickly as possible. She remembered pressing hard on the gas and that's when the car began to zig zag. They were going forward but she couldn't control the wheel and then she tried slamming on the breaks and that only made it worse. They continued to zig zag toward the edge of the embankment and there was nothing that she could do but scream.

By the time that she had told the story they were a long way from the accident site and her nerves were in a lot better shape. Bodie listened intently. He had reached out and held onto her hand. In that moment she didn't want him to let it go...even though it would be nice if he had both hands on the wheel.

"A vehicle wants to naturally right itself. If that should ever happen again, just release the wheel and the gas. If it's a real bad slide then you can try to gently turn the wheel but never jerk it."

He had squeezed her hand once again and then returned it to the steering wheel.

Riley was being very kind but she was still uncomfortable being under his roof. She just decided that she would be quiet and unobtrusive and let her son enjoy what was left of his Christmas with his dad.

Riley placed the tray on the bedside table and then gently lifted Adam and placed him on his own side of the bed. He pulled the covers up over him making sure that he placed his broken arm up over the covers. He did it with so much care that Stella's eyes began to glisten. She was reminded that she wasn't alone in this fight to protect Adam.

He took the tray and propped it on the bed before her. "It's just Campbell's soup. Nothing special. But this is a really good Virginia ham."

"Thanks Riley. I'm not sure if I can eat anything. My stomach is kind of queasy."

He sat down on the side of the bed and spooned soup towards her mouth.

"Uh...what are you doing?" She asked.

"Open," he said threatening to spill it down her mouth if she didn't quickly comply. She did.

"Good." He said. "One more." He spooned more soup into her mouth and then patted her lips with a cloth napkin.

She frowned at him. "That wasn't just a little weird."

He smiled. "That medicine is going to make you feel like crap if you don't have something on your stomach to act as a buffer."

He spooned more soup into her mouth. She almost pursed her lips together and turned her head away but at the last minute she decided that she liked the soup too much, so she opened her mouth for it.

She noticed that his knuckles were scratched and rubbed raw. He also had gashes on the pads of his palms. He was limping pretty bad too, but he didn't complain.

She reached out and took his hand and then she reached for the other. It looked like he had try boxing with a grizzly bear. "You got something for this?"

"It's alright." He said.

"Are you planning to take care of us?" Stella asked.

"That's my plan. Yes."

"Then you have to take care of yourself first. Go clean that and put a bandage on it."

He gave her a wry grin. "Fine. You eat the rest of that soup and at least half of the sandwich."

"Yes, sir."

He did as she requested. Someone knocked on the door when he was in the bathroom. He hurried down the stairs and looked out the window. It was Mrs. Jameson from up the road. What was she doing out in this weather.

He quickly opened the door and let her in. "Mrs. Jameson, you shouldn't be out in this ice."

"It's fine. I'm used to these roads and the snow stopped hours ago. Plus my daughter Alma is staying with me for Christmas and she drove." She was holding a bag in her hand and she handed it to him.

"Here. I made you all a casserole. It's just chicken and rice and some dinner rolls. Stella likes my lemonade so I made up a batch special for her." The pancakes that he'd made earlier were hockey pucks so he was grateful for the offer.

"That's nice. Thank you. Do you want to go up and say hi to her?" He asked, gesturing to the stairs.

"No. I don't want to disturb her. Tell her I'll stop in sometime later." She reached up and gave him a kiss on the cheek. "You're a good boy Riley Pranger. Thank God you were there to rescue Stella and Adam."

He gave her a surprised nod. "It all worked out good."

She patted his cheek and turned to leave but stopped. "Tell Adam that Brianna put a Christmas card in there for him. She's still in Cincinnati but when she heard that he was spending Christmas with you she mailed this to me to give to him."

"That's sweet. I'll give it to him when he wakes up."

When he went back upstairs he saw that Stella had finally fallen asleep. She had indeed finished off most of the soup and half the sandwich. He'd check in on her in a few hours and give her her next dose of pain medicine.

He checked on Adam who was sound asleep in just his undies and t-shirt. Peeking from beneath his shirt was his witch's finger. Bodie lifted it and placed it carefully on top of his shirt.

The rest of their possessions was still in the smashed up vehicle which Bodie had towed to the garage. He'd go down tomorrow to get their belongings. They at least had the cell phones, their coats and Stella's purse. But he had been too preoccupied to care about anything else. For a while he hadn't been sure that Stella would wake up. And hearing his son's cries of anguish had been nearly unbearable. But this Christmas he had a great deal to be thankful for. He thanked God in a silent prayer for giving him a Christmas with the most important gifts that he could ever wish for—the lives of his child and his child's mother.

Over the next few hours the doorbell rang several more times. Bodie came by carrying Adam and Stella's luggage and the gifts that they had brought to the mountain. Shaun had sent some children's aspirin since she was sure that Bodie wouldn't have any—and she was right.

Pastor Tim and first lady came with a toy for Adam and a lemon pie from Miss Birdie. Adam and Stella were awake by then and Stella thanked them for coming by on Christmas day in such bad weather. They only laughed and said that this wasn't anything near to the bad weather that they were used to.

After they left Pete came by with Jace. The toddler remembered playing with Adam over the summer and the two children sat together playing with Jace's puzzles.

"I'm happy that everything worked out for you." Stella said to Pete as they waited for Mrs. Jameson's casserole to heat up. Riley had planned on the ham and green beans with potatoes and onions and a dish of potato salad, but with all the commotion the only thing that was ready to eat was the ham.

So Mrs. Jameson's casserole was going to be Christmas supper tonight along with Mrs. Birdies lemon pie for dessert.

The handsome Mexican man gave her a wry, slightly sad smile. "It wouldn't have happened if not for the kindness of the people in Estill County," he said. "They surprised me. When I was at my lowest the people here rallied around me without me having to ask. People that I thought looked down their nose at me actually came to bat to keep me here. Even afterwards, they come in to the garage and they'd bring stuff for Jace, toys and clothes. Or they'll see me at the market or in town and give me stuff that they think might give me some help, a set of dishes, a crib, curtains."

He shook his head. "And Riley." The two of them were sitting on the couch watching the children play while Riley finished up in the kitchen with supper.

"He let me stay here rent free until I could get on my feet. And what he charges me is a steal. He told me that getting some rent is better then getting none, so I guess he's right."

Stella listened intently. She looked into the kitchen at the way Riley concentrated so intently on measuring the coffee to add to the coffee pot. She would have never expected so much kindness toward herself and for Pete—not from these people that she had just discounted to be little more than rednecks. She was a firm believer that you learn from what is right in front of your eyes and she knew that she had been wrong to judge these people so harshly.

"You planning on staying in Estill County?" She finally turned to Pete.

"I wouldn't live anywhere else."

Chapter Twenty-Nine

Riley didn't think that they would be up to it, but Adam wanted to celebrate Christmas so after supper they finally exchanged gifts. Riley had bought him a Louisville Slugger baseball bat, a baseball, and a baseball mitt. He also got two video games and a new gaming system.

Riley had also bought Jace a Nerf football, baseball and bat. Pete had been grateful for the unexpected gifts. Riley joked that he just wanted to make sure Little Jace didn't smash the television set with the real thing.

Riley opened the box that contained his gift. It was pretty banged up but the contents were undamaged. It was a new lunchbox, thermos, and a small cooler.

"Wow…" he said in surprise. It was actually a great gift. "Thanks. I'll definitely use these." He hugged Adam who looked at his mother proudly.

Pete and Jace left and while Adam gathered up the wrapping paper Riley retrieved the last gift which had been hidden in his Christmas stocking.

"I got something for you." He thrust the package to Stella who looked at him in surprise before accepting it.

"You didn't have to do that. I didn't get you anything."

Riley glanced over at the lunch equipment. It was Coleman brand and he was pretty sure that it was a gift from her as well as from Adam.

"It's nothing big. I just wanted you to have something to open on Christmas day."

"Thank you." She admired the professionally wrapped gift. She'd seen how Riley wrapped gifts and he sure hadn't done this himself. There was a fluffy pink bow on top. Perfect. She carefully opened it. There was a little jewelry box inside. She looked at Riley in surprise. Jewelry.

She opened the box and saw a locket inside. It was a silver heart and had an engraved S on front. She lifted it from the case. "It's beautiful," she said.

"Look inside." Adam came over then to see what she had. Stella opened the locket and saw a picture of Adam on one side. It was the school picture that she had sent him a few months ago but he'd gotten it shrunken down to fit. The picture on the other side brought a huge smile to her face. It looked like Riley at about the same age. She brought it closer and peered at the little image of Riley at Adam's age.

Adam wanted to see and they passed it back and forth. Riley finally took it and placed it around her neck.

Stella opened it again and stared at the two images. One had brown skin, the other had white but they were almost one in the same. She blinked back her tears.

"Mommy, why are you crying?" Adam asked.

Stella smiled and wiped away her tears.

"Are you okay?" Riley asked in concern.

"I'm okay. I just love my gift." She reached over and hugged Riley. "Thank you."

"You're welcome."

She whispered into his ear. "No. I mean thank you for helping me to see."

"See?" He asked hoping that she was referring to the only barrier that stood between them—not race, but their inability to find a common ground.

"We're all different," she continued, "but we're the same where it most counts."

He pulled back, still holding her in his arms—connected with her bodily. He looked at her as deeply as one can look at another. This time when the electrical zing passed between them, she didn't look away, which then connected them completely.

The next day Christmas Carolers knocked on the door—actual Christmas Carolers. Stella just stood there staring at them in astonishment. It seemed so sweet and yet so strange to have perfect strangers standing at the door singing to her.

Riley enjoyed it and simply listened silently with his arm comfortably around her waist and his other hand on Adam's shoulder. In that moment she felt like the family that she suddenly wished to be.

He thanked them and once they were gone he explained that they were from his church.

"This is the first year that I put my name on the list for carolers." It was the first time in years that he hadn't just sat in front of the television watching sports all day.

"How are you feeling this morning?" He asked her.

"Sore in places that I didn't know I had feeling."

"Well you should take it easy today. Bodie gave me the week off to spend with Adam, but I really should go in for a while. I want to take a look at your truck and get the pictures taken for the insurance assessors."

"It's fine. Adam and I will be alright."

He didn't really want to leave them but he knew how the insurance claims worked and he wanted to make sure that it was done quickly. He would only be away for a few hours. He thought about calling Mrs. Jameson to come down and check on them but he was being sill—Pete was right there.

"Well there's plenty of food and feel free to call me. I'll be home before dark."

He leaned in and kissed her lips lightly. He didn't ask and would take the slap across the face if she decided to deliver it. He had almost lost her and Adam and he wouldn't spend another wasted moment. Instead of slapping him she blinked in surprise and then with a soft sigh, wished him a good day.

He returned as quick as promised. Adam met him at the door and hugged him in relief. He closed the door and sat down on the little bench in the entranceway. He pulled Adam onto his lap and noticed his nails. He took hold of the boy's small hands, examining the nails that were bitten down to the cuticle beds and dotted with blood.

Stella came into the entrance. She sighed when she saw that Riley was examining Adam's nails. "He's been biting them again." He'd also sucked his thumb throughout the night again. And he'd had a wrestles sleep of tossing and turning.

Riley lifted his son and carried him into the living room. He sat on the couch with him on his lap.

"It's been a scary time, hasn't it?"

Adam nodded after a moment. "It's been fun here with you. The only thing that's been bad was the car accident."

Stella reached out and stroked his curly hair. She sat down next to him. "Adam, baby. You don't have to be afraid."

Adam looked off into the distance.

Riley gave him a gentle shake. "Hey buddy. What are you afraid of?"

"Nothing." Adam said softly. Riley looked at Stella who just shrugged slightly, but she was becoming worried. He caught sight of the small branch around Adam's neck. Riley touched it, his brow creasing. Why did his son feel that he needed to be protected?

"Adam. You know that you can open up to me about anything. I will listen to you no matter what you have to say. You know that, right?"

Adam nodded.

"I'm going to ask you a question and I want you to be honest. Okay?"

Adam nodded. "Okay, dad."

"What are you afraid of, son? You can tell me."

Adam touched his charm.

"Are you afraid of something?" Riley asked.

Adam slowly nodded his head.

"What is it, baby?" Stella asked. She wanted to cry or scream that something or someone had been scaring her child all this time and she hadn't known. "What is it baby?"

"I'm scared…" tears sprouted to his eyes and his lips began to tremble. "I'm scared that lady is going to take me away and that you won't be my mommy anymore." Suddenly he began to choke back sobs.

Stella looked surprised. "Do you mean your birth mother?"

Adam nodded. "I don't want her to take me away!"

Riley hugged him. "Oh, honey," he said. "Nobody's going to take you away from your mom. I won't let that happen."

"Adam, you've been worried about that all this time? Baby, she is not going to come and take you away. The judge made you *my* son. She has no more rights to you. Legally. She can never come back for you. And she doesn't want to do that. She wrote those letters so that you could talk to her when you are all grown up and only if you have any questions to ask her."

"But I don't have to talk to her, do I mommy?"

Stella stroked his hair and leaned in and kissed him. "No, baby. You don't ever have to see or hear from her. It's your choice."

Adam nodded, his tears disappearing. "I dream sometimes that she's going to come and make me go with her. Then I won't see you anymore."

Riley gave his son an earnest look. "If that ever happened I'll come and get you and take you right back to your mommy. Do you trust that?"

Adam smiled and nodded in relief. His daddy was a super hero. He could do anything. He even found him when he was lost in the woods. And he rescued them. Adam hugged his father.

After Riley put Adam into the bed that he was sharing with his mom, he closed the door, keeping the hall light shining to act as a night light.

Stella was wringing her hands anxiously. Riley took them in his. "It's alright, Stella."

"All this time…and I didn't know."

"You can't know everything." He led her down the stairs and poured her a glass of iced tea.

"You figured it out." She accepted the tea and took a long drink. "How?"

He sat down across from her at the large dining room table. "Because I did the same thing. I used to chew my nails down to the quick whenever I got stressed."

She gave him a worried look and then she took his hand and examined them. She looked at his palm. The bandage was still in place. She examined his nails. They weren't bitten down any longer. Adam would hopefully grow out of it too.

"What made you stressed as a little boy?" She asked.

Riley placed his other hand on top of hers and then examined her long fingers.

"I saw some things that a little kid shouldn't ever have to see."

She looked at him. "You didn't have it easy as a kid, did you Riley?"

He met her eyes. "No. But I knew a lot of people that had it worse. But you know something that I've learned?"

"What have you learned?"

He brought her fingertips to his lips and kissed each lightly. "I learned that if you don't speak up, life is going to lead you instead of the other way around."

She stared at the way he moved his lips over her fingers.

"I learned that I don't want to be passive any more—not in how I lead my life, not in how I handle my problems...and especially not when it comes to the mother of my child."

Her lips parted at the way his deep drawl rumbled from his throat. She looked up and into his eyes, hooded now and darker then she'd ever seen them before, yet still the eyes that he had given to her son—their son.

"Remember what I said to Adam?" He asked quietly. "That he could tell me anything. It's the same for you. You can say anything to me. Ask me anything. I will tell you whatever you want to know about myself, my past, my present—whatever it might be."

Stella looked down and realized that their fingers were intertwined. How could something so innocent, like fingers intertwined be so sensual? It was the contrast — and not just in color. Contrast — differences, weren't bad. His fingers were rough and calloused and hers slender and long. Hers caramel and his vanilla...Differences, contrast, light, dark...

She lightly nibbled her lip. "Okay." She replied.

"I want to give you all the time you need to get used to me." Riley leaned back in his chair causing her to realize that they had moved closer to each other. "But I intend to have you as my own. I want Adam but I also want you."

She blew out an amused breath. "You do, huh?"

He wasn't smiling. "Yep. Race is standing between us. And I don't want it to."

"Race is a big deal, especially in this day in age."

"It can be. But it doesn't have to be between us." He said.

She thought about her next words. "Did race play a role in why you broke it off with Jasmine?"

"No," he said. "I was just a dick." He rubbed the beard of his chin and looked off into the distance. "When I really understood that my careers as a football player was over, I pulled away from everything that reminded me of those dreams. I told myself that she would be better off without me, but if I'm honest with myself, I just didn't want to be reminded of all that I would never be." He met Stella's eyes.

"You asked me if I loved her. I did. But I was young and stupid. I thought that everything important about myself was lost with my knee injury. I didn't think a woman like her would want a man like me, not when I didn't have anything to offer."

"A man like you?" Stella asked while shaking her head. "What do you mean a man like you? Are you talking poor? A lot of people are poor, Riley. That doesn't make you less of a man."

He shook his head and looked away. When he met her eyes again they were filled with sadness. "Trash is what I mean. Poor. White. Trash."

She sighed and closed her eyes. Her hand found his again. When she opened her eyes they locked onto Riley's and he saw fire in them.

"Don't call my son's father that. Don't claim those words. I don't care what the rest of them think, but you don't claim those words."

He listened intently and thought about Sully. He never carried himself like trash, even when

Riley tried to convince him that he was. He bit his lip and nodded his head at her words.

"You're right."

"Let's agree not to use hate words, not towards ourselves and not towards others."

He nodded.

She sighed. "Then I agree...to give *us* a chance."

He blinked and then moved closer. She did the same until they were inches from each other.

"Kiss me like you did before." She whispered.

"Uh uh." He shook his head. And then his lips captured hers, the tip of his tongue chasing the kiss. He cupped her cheek, his fingers strummed along her jawline.

Stella caught her breath as a zing of electricity transferred between them.

"Did you feel that?" He whispered in amazement.

She nodded. "What was it?" she asked surprised that he could feel it too.

"Something right finally snapping into place."

She smiled. "I love how you say things."

He cupped her face again and this time when they kissed they didn't stop for a long time.

Chapter Thirty

Riley carefully lifted Adam from the bed. Stella watched from the hall, hoping that her son wouldn't wake up. He was normally a pretty hard sleeper. But when she wanted to love on his father, of course he would probably wake up. Riley held his breath and when it looked as if Adam would stay asleep he walked into the spare room. Stella quickly lowered the sheet and blankets and Riley placed him in his own bed. He tucked him in and then kissed his forehead.

The nightlight that he'd purchased earlier in the week was plugged in and it offered a soft glow within the neat room that had once been Riley's.

Stella slipped her hand into his and he looked over at her. She wore a t-shirt and pajama bottoms. Thick socks covered her feet and her hair was pulled up into a ponytail. She was the most beautiful woman that he'd ever seen.

She led him out of the room and into the master bedroom. Riley closed the door and then pulled off his shirt. Stella looked at his chest and then placed her hands on his shoulder. His hands went to her waist. They were nearly head to head. He'd never met someone that matched him so exactly.

He kissed her and she pressed her body against him, her curves molding with every chiseled plane and line of his. They were a perfect fit.

Riley allowed his fingers to scan her curves the way he had imagined doing so many times in the past.

Stella stepped back, reluctantly breaking the contact. She pulled off her shirt her breast full and tight from the sensations that his kiss had brought. Riley's erection surged to life as he took in her perfect form. He reached out and lightly touched the darkened bruises that had formed along her shoulder and across one breast. His fingers scanned the bruise until Stella began to tremble, her nipples forming hard nubs.

"Does this hurt?" He whispered.

"No," she shook her head. He came forward and trailed kisses down the bruises. He got down on his knees with just a small grimace and then he lightly kissed her belly and belly button.

She looked down and tried not to groan at the sight of his lightly shaved head and the feel of his beard and moustache on her delicate flesh.

"Riley..." she bit her lip and allowed her eyes to flutter close.

Riley cupped her ass and then dragged the fabric of her pajamas down until he was faced with the soft curls of her mound. He buried his face there searching for her scent, and once finding it becoming intoxicated by it.

Riley quickly came to his feet and led her to the bed. He wanted to taste her, to learn her unique flavor. Stella, with socks still on her feet but otherwise completely naked, lay on the bed with her knees drawn up. She watched him as he stood above her.

Riley pulled off his jeans and stood naked above her wearing only thick winter socks.

Stella came up on her elbows taking in every perfect inch of Riley Pranger. She reached out and he stepped closer so that she could touch is six-pack abs. She watched his eyes as she gripped his hard shaft. His knees almost buckled.

He gushed out some unintelligible words and quickly climbed onto the bed. He parted Stella's knees and settled in between them. He kissed her lips, and allowed his fingers to stroke her skin, circle her nipples, cup her mound and then glide along her slit...

His lips trailed down her body, following the exact path that his fingers had. When he reached her moist crease he lapped at it.

Stella gasped and squirmed. She spread her legs and held his head in place. Her hips rolled in small circles and Riley's tongue lapped and rolled in opposing ones.

She groaned suddenly and pushed Riley's head away. "Wait!" She cried.

Riley backed off, licking his wet lips and stroked his damp beard. Damn she tasted good.

Stella came up on her knees and pushed Riley down on the bed. She grinned lasciviously.

"I like this..." And then she gripped his cock and went down on him. Riley's eyes closed at the feel of her warm mouth on him, but when her tongue circled his sensitive head he shuddered and growled.

"I'm going to cum!"

She nodded her okay for him to cum. With a low growl, Riley came hard, his ejaculation slamming into her mouth and down her throat. He jerked his hips in time to the spurts, his fingers in her hair, holding her in place.

He growled something that sounded like a curse and a prayer. The moment he was finished without a pause he grabbed Stella and pulled her down on top of him.

"I'm not done with you yet!" He rolled her onto her back and once again spread her thighs. This time he sucked and lapped at her swollen clit, his chin and beard rubbing her sensitive inner folds until Stella could no longer hold the tremors that were engulfing her body.

With an explosive cry she climaxed into a series of convulsive seizures. Each time Riley touched her she would jerk uncontrollably. It was such a turn on for him to see her reaction to what he did with his tongue and mouth.

She panted and gave him a weary look when he smiled mischievously at her, one finger poised above her nipple.

She shook her head. "What are you doing?"

He lightly touched the beaded flesh and her body convulsed.

"Oh...damn." He whispered. "I'm hard again."

"Condoms..." she panted.

"I don't have any-"

"I do."

Riley's brow raised but he gave her a smile of appreciation.

"Will you hand me my purse?"

He quickly located her purse and handed it to her. There was a condom in her wallet. He liked that it appeared relatively old. It had been there for a while…

He tore it open and slipped it on. Stella pushed him down onto his back.

"Me on top."

Riley's brow rose in delight. He put his hand behind his head and watched Stella straddle his body. He quickly reached out to stroke her regal form. She was so tall and so statuesque. He covered her breast with his palms while she gripped his sheathed shaft from behind. She leaned forward and lined him up and then backed up allowing his cock to slip towards her opening.

With a groan of pleasure, Stella rose enough to impale herself on his stiff member. His cock forced her tight opening to part and make way for him. Stella cried out in pleasure. Riley reached down and stroked her clit with his thumb. He thrust upward gently, feeling her hot velvet interior squeezing and encasing him.

He hissed out a moan and continued to role and jerk his hips upward. He reached out with his other hand and gently pinched her swollen nipple causing her body to once again convulse and jerk.

He loved the way she reacted to his touch. He loved everything about her, her look, her smell and her taste. He loved her thoughts, her personality. He loved her honesty and her bravery. He loved her completely and totally.

"Stella..." he said with his final thrusts.

She collapsed on him. He felt so good beneath her, like an island. And he was big enough that she could lie on him and still allow her head to rest on his chest.

Riley felt the same. As he wrapped his arms around her he couldn't get over how perfectly she fit against him. He knew that her skin would feel like satin and he wasn't disappointed.

"You're perfect." He said.

She looked up at him. "Riley, don't you know how wonderful you are?"

He blushed and she kissed his neck. "I'll have to show you, I guess."

The next day Riley took them sledding. Stella had to watch them have all the fun since her body was still sore from the accident. But if Adam's wrist gave him any problems he didn't indicate it by the amount of whooping, shouting and running he did.

Stella loved watching her two fellas playing like little kids. Back at the house she made a quick lunch while Riley went out back to chop wood. Adam stayed inside with her instead of shadowing his father like he usually did. She figured he was just worn out from all of the activity. But he had a question for his mother. He had seen Stella and Riley share a brief kiss and hold hands as they walked to the hill where they had gone sledding.

"Mom?" He asked.

"Yes, sweetie?"

"Is…dad your boyfriend?"

She gave him a surprised look. "What?"

"You were holding his hand." Adam was blushing.

She lowered the flame beneath the skillet of burgers. "What would you think if your dad and I became girlfriend and boyfriend?"

He jumped up into her arms happily and squealed. "Can he live with us? Please mom?!"

She chuckled and kissed his cheek. "Let's not rush things. Okay? This is new for me."

"I know mom. You've never had a boyfriend before. But dad would make a great boyfriend."

She smirked in amusement. "Oh? Why do you think that?"

"Well he's strong. He beat up that bad man that time at the park. Also he never yells or fusses at me—even if I do something that I'm not supposed to. He looks at you funny, too."

"Funny? How?"

Adam giggled. "Like in the movies when Tony Stark wants to kiss Pepper Potts."

She smiled and turned back to the stove. "I'll tell you what, why don't you talk about it with your dad and see how he feels about it. If he's okay with it then…I guess it would be alright with me."

"Yes!" He jumped up and ran to the front door.

"Adam! No running in the house. And put on your coat!"

"Ok, mom!" She heard the door slam shut a few moments later. As she placed the finishing touches on the burgers the front door opened and Adam and Riley came in carrying logs for the fireplace.

Riley looked at her and grinned while she put on an innocent face.

"Go on Dad! Ask her." Adam whispered loudly.

"Well okay, can I take off my coat first?" Riley asked playfully.

"Ok." Adam said anxiously.

Riley hung up his coat and stuffed his skullcap and gloves into its pocket and then he unlaced his boots and placed them by the door. Adam was fidgeting next to him, whispering words of encouragement.

Stella could barely hold back her laughter. "You boys ready to eat? Lunch is ready."

"It sure smells good in here." Riley said while heading for the kitchen sink to wash his hands. Adam mimicked him and the two of them headed for their seats at the dining room table.

"Now dad!" Adam whispered.

"Okay okay." Riley watched her with a twinkle in his eyes. "Stella...uh...I was wondering..." he looked at his son for encouragement. Adam's eyes were bright as he nodded for his dad to continue.

Riley cleared his throat and then crossed to the other side of the table where Stella was sitting. She tried not to smile and to play it serious. He took her hand and looked deeply into her eyes.

"Stella." His eyes were suddenly serious. "Will you marry me?"

Her heart nearly leaped from her chest and her face went slack. She stood up and looked into Riley's eyes. For a moment she felt as if that magical connection between them had allowed her to momentarily swap places with him. It seemed as if part of her had slipped into him, and he into her and they were looking at each other through the other's eyes. When she blinked she saw her own eyes reflected back at her showing nothing but pure love.

"Is this for real?" She whispered.

He nodded.

She quickly nodded her head. "I'd be proud to be your wife Riley."

He inhaled a shaky breath. "Alright then." Riley pulled Stella into his arms and kissed her. Adam covered his eyes but his huge grin could still be easily seen.

Stella's arms went around Riley's neck and she held onto her big powerful mountain man.

Epilogue

~January 2018~

Pastor Tim placed a comforting hand on Riley's back. "She's in a better place, son."

"I just want her to be comfortable." Riley said hoarsely. He said that he wouldn't cry because this was Jewel Marlene Pranger's going home ceremony and he wouldn't look at it as her funeral. Hopefully now she would finally find rest.

Stella gripped his hand. He smiled at her thinking that she and Adam were the only family he had left—the only that he ever intended to recognize, that is. None of the other Prangers had shown up for the funeral not even his brother and sister. Both said that the weather was too bad but he knew the truth—they too had run away and cut themselves off from the bad memories on the mountain. And he didn't blame them for that.

Adam was standing at the casket looking at the matriarch of the Pranger family. Stella worried that the sight of the woman might give him nightmares but he said that he wanted to see his great granny at least one time. She decided that she couldn't deny him that request.

"Adam?" Stella called from the aisle. "Are you ready to go?"

"Yes." He gave the woman one last look and then headed for his mom and dad. Hidden beneath the sleeve of her dress and concealed by a bracelet of cheap white plastic was his witch's finger. He had placed it there careful not to allow it to peek out. He didn't need it anymore. His daddy was coming to live with them in the spring and his daddy was as strong and as tough as a super hero. Between him and his mom, nothing could ever hurt him.

But he did cast one last protective spell over his great granny so that she would be protected wherever she went next.

Back at home nearly everyone from the mountain came to pay their respects. Adam couldn't believe all the food that was in the kitchen, lined up on the dining room table and on the counters. There was even some of those green peas floating in that funny looking white sauce.

Brianna dared him to taste some but he refused. They went upstairs and played in his room. He had some new video games that she'd never seen.

Bodie and Shaun came with their three little girls. The littlest Matthew was named Madelyn and Stella stared down into her sweet little face while Bodie nudged Riley and warned him that it looked like Stella was planning on getting a few of them for herself.

"I hope." Was his response.

Mr. Dunwitty and Miss Lemon came from the market and brought a huge fruit basket. Dale and Bear from the barbershop showed up with a group of old timers that told some good stories about his granny. Mr. Epstein even slapped him happily on his shoulder and apologized for being a judgmental ass. Old man Connors from the post office snuck in a bottle of moonshine, but Christopher spotted it and poured it down the drain before Mr. Pete saw it. He had a hard time knowing when to stop.

Mr. Harper paid his respects and told Riley that he'd finally found someone trust-worthy to manage the hardware store. He told him that if he changed his mind about moving to Cincinnati— and if it didn't workout with Bodie he was always welcomed to come back.

Riley thanked him but told him that he had a job lined up working in an elementary school as a Phys Ed teacher. When Stella had first suggested it, he had almost told her that no one would want someone that sounded like him teaching their kids. But since he was sworn never to use the word *redneck* out loud he decided to consider it. Several schools were interested in him and would even help pay for him to complete the necessary college courses for him to get his Bachelor's degree.

Stella had proudly informed him that once they got married she would finally gain another stream of income.

He'd laughed. "You're losing one. No more child support, remember?"

It seemed that hundreds of people had come through the house but Riley was proud to have them. Once the last person had left he put away as much food as he could and ended up placing much of it in the stand-alone freezer when he ran out of room in the refrigerator.

"What are we going to do with all this food?" Stella asked once the last plastic container was placed neatly in the freezer.

"It'll be here when we come back to visit this summer."

"Ugh." Stella said.

"I'm kidding. I guess Pete and Jace won't need to cook for a while."

His renters were going to stay on in the little gingerbread cottage. Pete agreed to maintain the larger house for them in exchange for the reduced rent—although he was willing to do it for free. But Riley wasn't greedy. He just liked having the two streams of income—five now that he was marrying Stella.

Stella plopped down on the couch tiredly. Riley sat next to her, snuggling her neck. Adam had gone to the Jameson's to spend the night so they had the house to themselves.

"Thanks for coming down, sweetheart." Riley said while nibbling her earlobe. "I know you don't like driving up here in the snow."

"I don't mind driving in the snow, I'm just not taking that hill until spring." Pete had driven Riley down to Michael's buffet yesterday where they all had lunch and then Riley had driven Stella's brand new Lexus up the mountain. The insurance company had taken a look at the pictures—the ones taken by Riley all had blood in them, and hadn't balked about giving Stella a great payout.

Stella turned to him. "Are you sure you're not going to miss leaving Cobb Hill?"

He smiled. "I am going to miss it. I'm going to miss the way the leaves cover everything in autumn and the smell of the air. I'll miss the taste of the spring water in the summer. I'm going to miss fishing in Mr. Tennyson's lake, and listening to the people at the snake church hollering on Sundays. I'm going to miss Pastor Tim's sermons and trying to out run First Lady. I'm going to miss the ice cream at the Twin and the fried chicken at Michaels. I'm going to miss Miss Birdie's pies and seeing them old bag of bones sitting in the post office playing checkers." He nodded. "I'm going to miss Cobb Hill. But we aren't leaving it. We're going to be back."

The End

The Estill County Mountain Men Series

BEAST

Lt. Christopher Jameson's facial deformity leads him to a solitary life. Ashleigh's plus size leads her to self-esteem. Both discover the true definition of beauty in the modern day 'Beauty and the Beast' Fairytale.

A WRONG TURN TOWARDS LOVE

When Shaun takes a wrong turn into a dark mountain town, events turn dangerous involving the Klan, a broken down car and a sexy mountain man names Bodie.

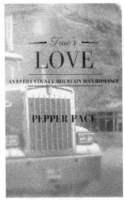

True's Love

When True handed over the last of her money at the bus station, she had no idea where she would land and how she would make due. Surprised that she was deposited in a sleepy mountain town that has evidently never seen a black person, True is determined to make this place home.

The Miseducation of Riley Pranger

When all you know is what you were taught by parents and friends that are ignorant to the world, you grow up to be a man like Riley Pranger, a passive racist and chauvinistic. But Riley is going to get a fast re-education

The Miseducation Of Riley Pranger

when a single black mother rents his home for the summer and he has no choice but to recognize the actions of the people around him.

Stella Burton is a no nonsense, 6-foot tall curvaceous black woman who has no problem with hurting a man's ego. She is opinionated, specifically about a country where she has been single handedly raising her multi-racial son to be a well-rounded black man.

What happens when white privilege is suddenly challenged? When races clash and you mess with the wrong black woman? This novella contains twists and turns and sexiness as well as appearances from Lt. Christopher Jameson, Ashleigh and their children from the novel Beast, Bodie and Shaundea Matthews from A Wrong Turn Towards Love and True from True's love.

The Miseducation Of Riley Pranger

Pepper Pace 'Heat' Index for Romances

Mild heat; Sweet romances. Contains some sexual tension but no graphic language or descriptions of sex. *May contain no sex acts.*

Moderate heat; Story driven with a small amount of sex, and or sex play. Mildly graphic sexual language.

Erotica; Sexually driven storyline. Strong language, graphic descriptions. No dubious sex, bondage or pain.

Hottest Sex; May include BDSM or taboo sex. Contains strong graphic language and descriptions of sex. No holds barred.

PEPPER PACE BOOKS

STRANDED!
Juicy
Love Intertwined Vol. 1
Love Intertwined Vol. 2
Urban Vampire; The Turning
Urban Vampire; Creature of the Night
Urban Vampire; The Return of Alexis
Wheels of Steel Book 1
Wheels of Steel Book 2
Wheels of Steel Book 3
Wheels of Steel Book 4
Angel Over My Shoulder
CRASH
Miscegenist Sabishii
They Say Love Is Blind
Beast
A Seal Upon Your Heart
Everything is Everything Book 1
Everything is Everything Book 2
Adaptation book 1
Adaptation book 2
About Coco's Room
The Witch's Demon book 1
A Bubble of Time
The Miseducation of Riley Pranger

SHORT STORIES
~~***~~

The Miseducation Of Riley Pranger

Someone to Love
The Way Home
MILF
Blair and the Emoboy
Emoboy the Submissive Dom
1-900-BrownSugar
Someone To Love
My Special Friend
Baby Girl and the Mean Boss
A Wrong Turn Towards Love
True's Love
The Delicate Sadness
The Shadow People
The Love Unexpected
The Vinyl Man
Punishment Island

COLLABORATIONS
~~***~~

Sexy Southern Hometown Heroes
Seduction: An Interracial Romance Anthology
Vol. 1
Scandalous Heroes Box set

Written under Beth Jo Andersen
~~***~~

Snatched by Bigfoot!
Bigfoot's Sidepiece
Mated to the Bigfoot!

Written Under Kim Chambers

~~***~~

The Purple World book 1

Sign-up to the Pepper Pace Newsletter!
http://eepurl.com/bGV4tb

About the Author

Pepper Pace creates a unique brand of Interracial/multicultural erotic romance. While her stories span the gamut from humorous to heartfelt, the common theme is crossing racial boundaries.

The author is comfortable in dealing with situations that are, at times, considered taboo. Readers find themselves questioning their own sense of right and wrong, attraction and desire. The author believes that an erotic romance should first begin with romance and only then does she offers a look behind the closed doors to the passion.

Pepper Pace lives in Cincinnati, Ohio where many of her stories take place. She writes in the genres of science fiction, youth, horror, urban lit and poetry. She is a member of several online role-playing groups and hosts several blogs. In addition to writing, the author is also an artist, an introverted recluse, a self proclaimed empath and a foodie.

Awards

Pepper Pace is a best selling author on Amazon and AllRomance e-books as well as Literotica.com. She is the winner of the 11th Annual Literotica Awards for 2009 for Best Reluctance story, as well as best Novels/Novella. She is also recipient of Literotica's August 2009 People's Choice Award, and was awarded second place in the January 2010 People's Choice Award. In the 12th Annual Literotica Awards for 2010, Pepper Pace won number one writer in the category of Novels/Novella as well as best interracial story. Pepper has also made notable accomplishments at Amazon. In 2013 she twice made the list of top 100 Erotic Authors and has reached the top 10 best sellers in multiple genres as well as placing in the semi-finals in the 2013 Amazon Breakthrough Author's contest.

9 781984 010605